Readers Love ANDREW GREY

Through the Flames
"What a beautiful story of hate turning to love and putting the past where it belongs…. Sex, lies, suspense and forgiveness made this a must-read book."
—Paranormal Romance Guild

Only the Brightest Stars
"It's a story of patience, of kindness and of facing your demons. These two deserve their happy ending."
—Sparkling Book Reviews

Heartward
"Each aspect of this story gives great insight and depth to the characters, which just added to the chemistry I felt on the page between the two men."
—MM Good Book Reviews

Homeward
"Getting to figure out how to make a real relationship is not an easy path, but one they are willing to work at. Recommended for fans of couples reunited after many years and finally figuring out their lives."
—Love Bytes Reviews

By Andrew Grey

Published by DREAMSPINNER PRESS
www.dreamspinnerpress.com

By ANDREW GREY (cont'd)

CARLISLE DEPUTIES
Fire and Flint
Fire and Granite
Fire and Agate
Fire and Obsidian
Fire and Onyx
Fire and Diamond

CARLISLE FIRE
Through the Flames

CARLISLE TROOPERS
Fire and Sand
Fire and Glass
Fire and Ermine

CHEMISTRY
Organic Chemistry
Biochemistry
Electrochemistry
Chemistry Anthology

COWBOY NOBILITY
The Duke's Cowboy
The Viscount's Rancher

DREAMSPUN DESIRES
The Lone Rancher
Poppy's Secret
The Best Worst Honeymoon Ever

EYES OF LOVE
Eyes Only for Me
Eyes Only for You

FOREVER YOURS
Can't Live Without You
Never Let You Go

GOOD FIGHT
The Good Fight
The Fight Within
The Fight for Identity
Takoda and Horse

HEARTS ENTWINED
Heart Unseen
Heart Unheard
Heart Untouched
Heart Unbroken

HEARTWARD
Heartward
Homeward

HOLIDAY STORIES
Copping a Sweetest Day Feel
Cruise for Christmas
A Lion in Tails
Mariah the Christmas Moose
A Present in Swaddling Clothes
Rudolph the Rescue Jack Russell
Secret Guncle
Simple Gifts
Snowbound in Nowhere
Stardust
Sweet Anticipation

LAS VEGAS ESCORTS
The Price
The Gift

LOVE MEANS...
Love Means... No Shame
Love Means... Courage
Love Means... No Boundaries
Love Means... Freedom
Love Means ... No Fear
Love Means... Healing
Love Means... Family
Love Means... Renewal
Love Means... No Limits
Love Means... Patience
Love Means... Endurance

LOVE'S CHARTER
Setting the Hook
Ebb and Flow

Published by DREAMSPINNER PRESS
www.dreamspinnerpress.com

By ANDREW GREY (cont'd)

MUST LOVE DOGS
Rescue Me
Rescue Us
Rudolph the Rescue Jack Russell
Secret Guncle

NEW LEAF ROMANCES
New Leaf
In the Weeds

PAINT BY NUMBER
Paint By Number
The Northern Lights in His Eyes

PLANTING DREAMS
Planting His Dream
Growing His Dream

REKINDLED FLAME
Rekindled Flame
Cleansing Flame
Smoldering Flame

SENSES
Love Comes Silently
Love Comes in Darkness
Love Comes Home
Love Comes Around
Love Comes Unheard
Love Comes to Light

SEVEN DAYS
Seven Days
Unconditional Love

STORIES FROM THE RANGE
A Shared Range
A Troubled Range
An Unsettled Range
A Foreign Range
An Isolated Range
A Volatile Range
A Chaotic Range

STRANDED
Stranded
Taken

TALES FROM KANSAS
Dumped in Oz
Stuck in Oz
Trapped in Oz

TALES FROM ST. GILES
Taming the Beast
Redeeming the Stepbrother

TASTE OF LOVE
A Taste of Love
A Serving of Love
A Helping of Love
A Slice of Love

WITHOUT BORDERS
A Heart Without Borders
A Spirit Without Borders

WORK OUT
Spot Me
Pump Me Up
Core Training
Crunch Time
Positive Resistance
Personal Training
Cardio Conditioning
Work Me Out Anthology

Published by DREAMSPINNER PRESS
www.dreamspinnerpress.com

ANDREW GREY

THE NORTHERN LIGHTS IN HIS EYES

DREAMSPINNER PRESS

Published by

DREAMSPINNER PRESS

8219 Woodville Hwy #1245
Woodville, FL 32362 USA
www.dreamspinnerpress.com

The Northern Lights in His Eyes
© 2024 Andrew Grey

Cover Art
© 2024 L.C. Chase
http://www.lcchase.com
Cover content is for illustrative purposes only and any person depicted on the cover is a model.

Trade Paperback ISBN: 978-1-64108-678-3
Digital ISBN: 978-1-64108-677-6
Trade Paperback published July 2024
v. 1.0

To the memory of my Aunt Marilyn. Her life at Willow and the time we spent there together inspired this story.

CHAPTER 1

GARVIN HARVERTON woke knowing something wasn't right, but damned if he could figure out what. He had a knack for things sometimes, which meant whatever it was would reveal itself in time, or maybe it was just his imagination running on overtime. Still, it made him wonder what was in store for him.

The electric clock with battery backup glowed that it was almost seven in the morning, but it was still almost completely dark. He got out of bed and slid his feet right into heavy slippers before making his way to the wood stove in the next room. He'd been up in the middle of the night to add more fuel, but he didn't remember doing it. The action had become a habit after the hundreds of times he'd done it over the years. Heck, Sasha, his Samoyed, who slept near his legs, never raised his big head. At least when he flicked the switch near the door, the lights came on. That was an improvement over the past few days at least. He had a propane heater and used it to provide a base level of heat in the house, but anything above that came from the wood he felled, cut, split, and stacked beside his cabin. Garvin added more wood to the stove, and the fire flared to life. That was one chore done. He scratched his backside and headed for the bathroom.

All the pipes that ran under the cabin were well insulated to keep them from freezing, though it did happen on occasion. But as long as he kept the house warm, he was generally okay. Fortunately, this morning he even had hot water, and he relished a very quick hot shower. Then, after shaving, brushing his teeth, and checking to make sure his hair didn't look like Grizzly Adams's, he left the bathroom door open so heat could circulate. He dressed quickly, fed Sasha, and made a rough but hearty breakfast of oatmeal with some bacon and the last of the ham. Ready for the day at just before eight, he logged on to his computer, brought up the conferencing application, and watched as, one by one, bleary-eyed kids logged on for school.

Sasha poked his head into the camera frame and got greetings from Garvin's students before lying near his feet.

These were bush kids. They lived with their families in the rough wilderness areas of the state. Garvin worked with their parents and state officials to help ensure that they got an education. The faces were familiar, but always seemed to vary, since the kids were spread over a wide area and sometimes had power issues, just like he had had the past couple of days. Still, Garvin went through the lesson, making it as engaging as possible. He always assigned homework of a sort, and the kids emailed it in or sent him pictures of their artwork and stuff. At the end of the day, he said goodbye and signed off. Before getting up from his desk, he made sure that he had the rest of his lessons planned and sent his missing students a link to the recording of their class. They would need to watch it and complete the work once they were able to. He also graded all the assignments he had and sent them back before feeding the fire again and making sure the stove was closed up. It had been days since he had seen anyone in person, and he was starting to go a little stir-crazy.

"Do you want to go to the trading post?" he asked Sasha, who perked up immediately. Aside from the part where he greeted the kids, class held no fascination for his dog, but the trading post did. "Then let's get ready."

Garvin got out his winter gear and dressed in layers that started with thermal underwear. By the time he was in his heavy snow pants and parka, Sasha was prancing at the door. He knew the routine and was anxious for some fun. After checking that the fire was banked, Garvin left his home and started the snowmobile, then climbed on. Sasha was ready to go, and they took off with Sasha running behind him.

Garvin's cabin was one of less than two dozen on the road around the south side of Willow Lake, about seventy miles north of Anchorage. The road itself was covered in snow but had been plowed recently, so he and Sasha had a relatively easy trip. They made it to the main road and then went left to travel a quarter mile before turning into the trading post. Garvin parked next to four other snowmobiles and headed inside.

Warmth assaulted him, and he pulled off his heavy outerwear and hung it on one of the hooks near the door.

"Afternoon, Garvin," Angie called. She managed the trading post bar and always greeted him with a smile. "I have some fresh moose stew if you want some." She looked over the bar. "Sasha, go find your place."

Sasha loped around to the corner and lay down in the dog bed. Most dogs in the area were working ones and didn't come inside. Angie made an exception for Sasha.

"Sounds good," Garvin said as he took a stool at the bar. He ordered himself a light beer and settled in for a few hours of community news and fellowship. "Thank you."

"No problem." She got his beer, then headed to the back and returned with a large bowl of hearty stew that smelled amazing. Out here in the cold north, it took a lot of calories to keep a body going. The first bite warmed Garvin from the inside out. There was nothing bland about this stew. Angie always added a little chili, so it had a kick of heat to add to the warmth.

"What's new?" he asked, looking around.

"Claire is having another of her library nights on Tuesday. Supposed to be clear, so it could be a good aurora viewing," Joe said from next to him. They were neighbors of a sort, though if Garvin thought about it, nearly everyone was a neighbor out here in one way or another.

"I'll think about coming up." Lord knows he needed to get out every once in a while. "You know what that's about?" He nodded toward where Enrique and his partner, Devon, were talking to a state trooper off in the corner.

"Nope," Joe said and turned back to his beer. "Fucking winter. Sometimes I look forward to it, and then I remember how damned cold it is and I wish...."

Garvin laughed. "That you went to Florida?" It was an old joke. Every February for the past few years, Angie threw a big tropical-themed bash just to try to coax the sun and a little warmth farther north, if only in their minds. "Been there, done that, bought the T-shirt." Garvin finished his stew and then downed the last of his beer before slipping off his stool to wander over.

"Hey, Devon." He shook hands with the man who to the outside world was a famous artist, but to all of them was another member of their year-round community.

"Garvin, did you see anyone on your way in? Trooper Nelson here found a car."

"Abandoned a few miles south. No driver, which means they got out, and God knows how far they made it. Worst thing possible to try to make it out on foot out there." Especially since it was twenty below last night and it wasn't going to warm up much. "Just hoping you might have seen something."

"No, sorry. Sasha didn't either, or he would have reacted. And I didn't see footprints heading toward any of the summer cabins. Are you going to organize a search party?"

"We can't. There's another front heading in. The temperature is supposed to rise, but that means plenty of snow and wind, so visibility is going to be terrible," Enrique explained. "We'll all keep our eyes open, but there isn't much any of us can do."

"I'll take a drive back down that way, see if I can find anything. I was hoping he might have wandered in here and found shelter. There isn't much out where we found the car." The trooper stood. "It's possible they called for help and someone picked them up, but I thought I saw the remnants of a trail in the snow. After the wind last night, it's hard to tell."

"We'll call if we find out anything," Enrique said, standing when the trooper did. "Get yourself a mug of coffee to go."

"Thanks." The trooper stopped at the bar, got his coffee, and headed out into the afternoon. The sun had barely made an appearance and would set again in a few hours. It was nearly one, and by five it would be dark again. Just one of the joys of Alaska—the sun barely set in summer and barely rose in the winter.

Garvin sat down with Devon, and Sasha wandered over and sat next to him, leaning against his leg.

"There are times when I wonder why I put up with all this cold," Devon said. "Then it warms, the snow melts, and spring bursts into life and color like nowhere else on earth. All the beauty gets packed into a few months, so it puts on one hell of a show."

"You working on anything right now?"

Devon nodded. "I've got about four things going. One I need to finish soon, and the others I've gotten started, but I need to wait for spring to finish them. I want to capture that moment when everything bursts out all at once. I started them last year and ran out of time. Why? You need something?"

"Yeah. My kids are as cooped up as we are, so I thought that maybe a special art lesson would be fun. Maybe with a little art history thrown in. It would be online, so we could do it from your studio. The kids would love to see that."

"Sounds good. Set it up and we'll do it." Devon was always great to work with. He leaned over to Enrique, sharing a smile and a gentle pat on the shoulder. Garvin looked away, not because he was embarrassed, but to give them a little privacy and to tamp down the swell of jealousy. They were good friends of his. He wasn't attracted to either man, though they were handsome. It was the fact that they had found each other out here and were building a life together. Garvin had had that once, seven years ago, before Alaska... but a defect in John's brain that had been there since birth had taken him away, leaving Garvin alone in little more than the time it took to flip a light switch.

Devon stared at Enrique for a few seconds, almost as if he were seeing to the core of him. Then, without a word, he went on through to the back, where he had his studio, and closed the door quietly. Garvin had seen that look enough to know it meant that inspiration had struck.

"Four hours," Joe said from the bar and pulled out a tablet. Multiple five-dollar bills settled on the bar as others called out times. Apparently they were starting a pool on how long Devon's work jag would last.

"I'll take six."

"Hah, only three. Then he'll lose the light and stop," Jessup added, tossing in his five.

"Guys...," Enrique said, hitting them with a glare.

"Come on. We've got to have some fun," Joe said, and Enrique shook his head. "If anyone needs supplies or wants to place orders, you need to get them to me in the next hour." He sat down at his desk, and Garvin pulled out his list of goods. He got them and paid, trying to decide if he wanted another beer before heading home. He settled for a water and sat in one of the chairs in the side room with Sasha resting his head on his lap. After finishing his drink, he started the process of putting on his gear. Then he got his supplies, said goodbye to everyone, and he and Sasha headed out into the growing twilight. He stowed his supplies in the insulated box strapped to the back of the snowmobile and started the engine, and then he and Sasha headed for home.

Garvin went at a moderate speed, with Sasha easily keeping up. That dog loved being outdoors, and the cold had no effect on him. By the time they reached the cabin, the sky had purpled and the first stars began coming out… and it was still just after five. Garvin put the snowmobile next to the overhang for the ATV and his four-wheel-drive. Sasha stood at the edge of the yard, staring off into the trees. Garvin followed his gaze and then shook his head. "Come on, boy. Let's get where it's warm."

Sasha turned away and headed to the door. Garvin let him inside and got the supplies before following him. He closed the door and took off his outer gear. Before getting too comfortable, he built the fire back up and put some water on the propane stove to heat. As the room began to warm, he slipped off another layer before feeding Sasha and making sure he had plenty of water.

Garvin expected Sasha to lie down and nap for a while, but he hurried to the door and sat there as though he expected something to happen. The dog sat there for a few minutes, then came over, whined a few times, and hurried back to the door. Garvin didn't want to go back outside, but he knew well enough that something had upset Sasha. After pulling on his coat, he opened the door and stepped outside just in time for a man to stumble under the carport and collapse onto the ground.

"Sasha, get back inside." Garvin hurried to the man, got him up, and lifted him into his arms. He was almost more than Garvin could carry, but he managed to get him inside and the door closed.

Every bit of skin he could see was red. He peeled the coat, which was too thin for this kind of cold, off of him and then laid him on the sofa by the fire. "Can you hear me?" Garvin asked.

"Yes," the man answered before shivering violently. Garvin knew that shivering and movement were the body's way of trying to warm itself, so that was a good sign. He took off the man's gloves and hat, groaning when he got a good look at his features. He had never expected to see that face again, and now the ass had nearly gotten himself frozen to death.

"That's good. Now, when you can talk, you can tell me what the hell you're doing out here and what you thought you were doing traipsing through the damned woods."

"I came here to try to find you," William said, and all Garvin could do was shake his head.

"Why?" He probably should be concerned about whether William had frostbite, but he was more worried about why he was here and what he might have brought along with him, figuratively speaking. William had a habit of getting himself into trouble. He never meant for things to happen, but they did, and it always seemed to catch William by surprise and affect the people around him. Before moving north, Garvin had cut ties, and he thought he had made a clean break from William.

"I wanted to see you." William continued shivering.

Garvin spread a blanket over him. "You need to lie down and stay still. Let your body warm up gradually." Even though he wanted answers, now wasn't the time to press. Leaving William on the sofa, he made some tea and brought William a mug. "Sip this. It will help warm you on the inside. Take a few drinks, but not too much all at once."

William's hands shook a little as he took the mug and sipped. "I thought I was going to die."

Garvin looked into William's eyes. They had once been close friends, but Garvin had needed a break from him. "You came very close to it. Was it your car that broke down on the main road?"

William nodded and took another sip of the tea, shaking less as his body warmed. "Yes. I knew I was close, so I used my phone to lead me here. But I guess it was so cold the battery died. I tried to remember the right direction and kept going. I followed the road part of the way but thought the woods would be faster."

Typical William. He floundered his way into a situation, made all the wrong decisions, and hoped he'd come out all right. "You should never leave your car like that, not up here. The police would have found you hours ago and helped you. They were in the trading post looking for you earlier today." Garvin shook his head, trying not to show his frustration and annoyance at this man.

The thing was that William had the eyes of an angel, and his innocent face had everyone thinking he needed their help. William knew it all too well and played on that. He could slip into the "help me" act faster than anyone Garvin had ever known. "I know that now. I thought I could get here, and I didn't realize how cold it really was until I had gone part of the way, and then everything started to hurt. I walked faster, hoping to make it, and…." He lowered his gaze. "My feet really hurt."

Garvin sighed. "Okay. Let's get these wet clothes off so the heat can get to you." He only hoped William hadn't gotten frostbite or worse. There was still something about William that made Garvin want to help him, and as angry as he was for falling into old habits, he couldn't just leave the guy on his own. "I'll get you something warm and dry to wear." He left the room as William undressed. He reached his bedroom door before glancing back, groaning to himself because he told himself he wasn't going to look, and yet here he was, staring at the bare backside of the man he knew he should not be looking at, no matter how stunning he was.

CHAPTER 2

WILLIAM MOVED slowly, his hands and feet aching as feeling returned. He figured he should count himself lucky that it was. The fact was that he had almost died out there. The woods had been foreign and a lot thicker than he had expected, and the cold had been a lot more insidious than he had ever imagined. William had thought that he could outrun it somehow, that if he kept moving and pulled his hands and arms in, he could keep it at bay long enough to reach safety. But he was so wrong. The cold never stopped working its way through his clothes, and it became apparent after a while that it was only a matter of time. If William wanted to survive, he needed to find help. That and the fact that he knew Garvin was out there ahead of him were the only things that kept him going forward. He supposed he'd been lucky that there hadn't been wind, but then eventually it hadn't mattered. The cold still worked its way in, even as William closed each hole in his defenses, wrapping his face in his scarf until his eyes peered out between the layers of fabric, his hat pulled as low as he could get it, hands tucked into his sleeves, even the bottom of his coat pulled closed around his waist. He'd done everything… and the cold still crept in.

By the end, he had almost given up hope. The sun was setting, and William knew that he was running out of options… and it only got colder and darker.

Then he saw it, the light between the trees. It flashed on and off as he moved, but William hadn't been able to figure out why. All he knew was that light meant people. He forced himself forward, breaking out of the trees and into a slot without snow just as his numb feet went out from under him. He fell, but he felt nothing. For a second he'd wondered if he was dead, and then he heard that voice, the one he'd been looking for… and he wondered if he was in heaven. Then he was inside, and the cold abated. He could breathe again, and the familiar voice of the person he'd been so desperately looking to find grew hard and sharp… and he wondered if he was in hell.

William hissed softly as he pulled off his clothes and the heat from the room met his bare skin. He still felt cold, but once he got out of what he'd been wearing and into fresh clothes, the warmth reached more deeply inside. After a few more sips of tea, he sat back down on the sofa and pulled the blanket Garvin had given him over himself. Then he started shivering again, only this time not because of the cold but because he had nearly died, and because he had made stupid decisions yet again.

He wanted to sink into the cushions and disappear from sight. William had come up here because he had decided he wanted to live his life better and be the person he knew he could be. Garvin had always been the one guy who made him want more from himself, the one who saw William as something more than just a club kid with cotton fluff between his ears. But maybe that was what he really was—some fuckup who would never be anything beyond his looks: pretty but stupid.

"Are you warming up?" Garvin asked brusquely, and William nodded. "Finish the tea. It will continue helping you get warm, and you need fluids. The cold air is very dry." He went to the kitchen while the large dog hefted himself up onto the sofa. William tensed, watching the gargantuan creature as he stretched out, taking most of the room.

"When did you get the small horse… err, dog?" He watched the animal, wondering if he was sizing up William as his next meal.

Garvin chuckled. "He was the one who saved you. Sasha heard you outside and got me to go out." He returned with a mug of tea for himself and sat down. "And technically, you're in his spot." Garvin called the dog, and Sasha got down and went over to sit by his chair. Garvin stroked him, and Sasha leaned in for more attention. "So why did you come all this way? Willow is a long way from West Hollywood."

"I could ask you the same question," William countered. "You said you were coming up here to try to figure some things out, but then you left and we never really heard much from you again." William had found that confusing.

"That's because West Hollywood wasn't my life. I went there to try to get away from memories that followed me everywhere I went." Garvin was always so wrapped up in trying to figure out something about himself. Or maybe he was just trying to run away. William could never figure it out.

"But you had friends there," William said.

Garvin rolled his eyes. "I met people there. West Hollywood was like living in a fantasyland. There were guys everywhere, and they all looked over their shoulders in case they saw someone hotter and more interesting than the guy they were with at that moment. It was fun for a while, but I needed something else." He sighed, sipped his tea, and grew quiet, which infuriated William. "I was with a lot of guys, and none of them…."

William set his nearly empty mug on the side table. "Were John." He knew that refrain well enough to be able to finish the tune. The entire time William had known Garvin, he had screwed a ton of guys, but he never got serious about any of them because they didn't measure up to his dead lover. It was the one thing William always knew about Garvin and the one reason he never got involved with him—physically, anyway— even though William swore the first time he laid eyes on Garvin that the gods had made that man for him. Too bad no one else ever thought that, including Garvin. "And have you found what you're looking for here?"

Garvin didn't answer. "You need to get some rest. I'm going to make something to eat." He got up, and William watched him leave the room, tension rolling off him in a constant flow like evening ocean fog over the coastal hills. William pretended not to see Garvin's anxiety. He was good at that sort of thing. Lots of his friends thought he was kind of dumb. He'd heard them talking when they thought he couldn't hear. Garvin had never done that, even when William messed things up all to hell and needed to be bailed out yet again.

The kitchen was in the one corner of the cabin, and as soon as Garvin got to work, Sasha came back over and jumped up on the couch once more. "You're not going to attack me, are you?" Sasha blinked at him like he was crazy. Then he plopped his enormous head in William's lap. "Maybe you're smelling me to try to figure out how good I'm going to taste."

"Or he wants you to rub his head because he's looking for attention," Garvin said, and William gently patted the dog's head. "Sasha is a good dog. He hasn't eaten anyone in at least a month."

"Har-har." William stroked down Sasha's head and over his back. "That's not funny." Especially with how his heart was racing a mile a minute.

11

"He's a really good dog, and he isn't going to hurt anyone," Garvin clarified. "I got him just after I moved up here. One of the guys' dogs had a litter, and Sasha was the runt. They gave him to me, and it's pretty much been the two of us ever since." He continued working in the kitchen, and William relaxed a little as he petted Sasha, letting go of his anxiety until the huge dog stood on the cushions, turned in a circle, and lay down next to him, his back pressed tightly against William's side.

"What was that for?" William asked.

"He knows you're cold, so he's trying to warm you up. It's part of their pack mentality. These are dogs bred for the cold, and part of how they survive is to group together. If you're cold, his instinct is to try to warm you, and he can generate a lot of heat."

William nodded. Now that he was warm, fatigue set in big-time, and he could barely keep his eyes open.

Garvin brought over a sandwich on a small plate and placed it in his hands. "Eat this. The cold saps all your energy. I'm still heating up dinner." He returned to the kitchen, and William wolfed down the turkey sandwich in a few bites, kicking in his appetite, which was ravenous.

"Thank you… for everything." He set the plate on the table and sat back, feeling more than a little stupid.

"How did your car break down?" Garvin asked.

"I hit some ice, I think, and ended up in a snowbank. I think I'd rather drive in LA traffic. There was no one else anywhere, and I figured that if I didn't try to get some help on my own, no one was going to find me."

"Well, it's winter, and while people do travel, we're gearing up for a storm in the next few days." As if to punctuate the point, the wind whistled outside. "Though tonight should be clear, and if we're lucky…." William wandered over to the window as streaks of green, yellow, and even touches of blue and red appeared in the sky.

"Is that the aurora?" William asked, feeling as well as hearing when Garvin drew near to him. He had always had this sense of whenever Garvin was close, and he could almost feel him, as if he were actually touching him.

"Yes. It doesn't happen every night. Only when solar activity has been enough to trigger it. But yeah, that's it." His voice was soft and gentle. "There are many cultures where it's considered good luck to make love under the aurora. Some of them even say that a child conceived under the aurora will be charmed and that they are destined for great things."

They grew quiet as the lights danced and undulated across the sky. "I've never seen them before. I always wanted to." He wanted to take Garvin's hand. This seemed like a special moment, and William couldn't look away. He found himself leaning toward Garvin, but William straightened up again. William turned toward Garvin and found him looking back, watching him. Their gazes locked, and William's pulse raced a little faster.

William shivered with excitement, but Garvin stepped away to add more wood to the stove. "It's going to get even colder tonight because of how clear it is." He closed the stove door and returned to the kitchen, leaving William at the window to watch the aurora alone.

WILLIAM FINISHED the last of the hearty soup that Garvin had heated up for dinner. He was finally warm and full. His hands and feet had stopped tingling, and while his skin was still red, at least none of it had turned black.

"I think you owe me an explanation," Garvin told him. "And don't be surprised if the police stop by tomorrow. I called to let them know that the person they were looking for had been found and that he was physically okay." That glare told William a lot.

"You're angry with me," William said.

Garvin shook his head. "Of course I am. You fly all the way up here, rent a car, which you abandoned in the snowbank, and then nearly get yourself killed by traipsing through the woods in ten-below weather in order to find me. What I really want to know is why. I left West Hollywood almost two years ago."

William shrugged off Garvin's anger. "I know you're upset because you're worried, and I know that you care." He wasn't sure what reaction he expected, but Garvin ground his teeth and his eyes blazed. William thought it was kind of cute. Not that he liked making Garvin angry, but at least the guy was feeling something.

"Of course I do. But I've built a new life here—"

William leaned over the table. "And you think, what? That your old life and those of us who care about you just didn't matter anymore? You announced one day that you were leaving… and then poof, you were gone and we didn't see you anymore. You sold the house you and John had, and then a few days later you were off to Alaska. Did you figure that we just stopped existing… or maybe we didn't matter to you? Or was it John's memory that didn't matter to you?"

Garvin smacked his hands down on the tabletop, making Sasha jump and hurry over to him. "I left because I couldn't take it anymore. John had been gone five years and I wasn't healing. I should have been, but I couldn't. John was everywhere—in the place where I lived, in the things I was surrounded by. Every day I went to bed and woke up to the things that were part of our lives together. I tried cleaning out parts of the house, but he was everywhere, even in all of my friends. So I decided to try to build a new life. My aunt Susan and her second husband built this place, and she left it to me when she passed away. So…."

"You decided to come up here and live in a summer cabin all year long. It was like you dropped off the face of the earth. We never heard from you, and some of us…." William felt his own anger rising. "Some of us really cared for you—still care for you—and you just flew away like some bird and never returned."

"It's been almost two years," Garvin repeated.

William drew his lips into a harsh line, glaring at Garvin. "And you think that we're going to stop caring for you, stop loving you, just because of a matter of months?" Okay, he was exaggerating the time, but Garvin's departure had left a hole in William that he didn't know how he was supposed to fill.

"Almost two years—"

"Potato, po-tah-to," he countered and realized he sounded like a kid having an argument with his father.

"Let me get this straight. You came all the way up here and nearly died… for what exactly? What did you have to say to me that you couldn't have just picked up the phone for?" Garvin's eyes blazed with what might have been confusion or anger. William wasn't sure.

"You don't get it, do you?" William asked. "You never got it. After John died, there were plenty of us who were there for you. We stayed with you and made sure you didn't feel like you had lost everything, even though we missed him too. John was also my friend, you know. I knew him before I knew you. He was the best man I ever knew, and then he was gone, poof, just like that." William realized he was saying *poof* a whole lot in this conversation, but it fit, and every time he did, Garvin's expression softened a little. "We—I missed him too. The same way you did, and I thought…." Maybe he was stupid. People seemed to think that about him, so maybe it was true.

"That still doesn't explain why you made this whole trip up here. I have email, or you could have called."

"Because if I did, you would have blown me off just like you did Shawn. He sent you emails and texts, and you never answered. We figured you were being an ass and shit. He gave up. But I knew where you were. I had the address of this place, so I decided to come up here and brave the elements like some gayboy yeti so I could see you and actually talk to you." William sighed, but he refused to back down. If he was stupid, so be it, but at least he'd acted based on his heart.

"Okay, you wanted to see me. But there are easier ways and ones that don't involve risking your life. And for the record, I never got anything from Shawn. I live out where things are rough, and I had to change a lot of things in my life. But still—"

William stood up and looked down at Garvin. "You want to know why I came all this way? Why I tried to walk all the way here?" He walked around the table and stood next to Garvin. When Garvin angled his head up to look at him, William thought about punching the man in the fucking nose just because he was being such an ass. But William had come all this way… and what the fucking hell. He'd do what he needed to… so he leaned down and kissed Garvin with every damned ounce of energy he had.

CHAPTER 3

"WHAT DO you think you're doing?" Garvin asked once he could think straight again. William had kissed him, and instantly his mind had shut down all his thoughts, and his reasoning had skipped like an old-fashioned record. What was worse, he actually found himself kissing William back, because damn, he tasted good, smelled better, and…. But no. He couldn't do this. He was not going to do something as stupid as this… with anyone.

"I'm showing you why I came all this way." William didn't back away, and he didn't show the least sign of contrition. "I came here to tell you that I haven't forgotten you and—"

"To kiss me? Was this some way of saying that you've been secretly in love with me all the years you've known me? Did John know how you felt?"

William rolled his eyes. "For God's sake, get over yourself. I wasn't pining for you when John was alive. You two were so in love, and everyone could see it. John was my friend, and so were you." He stayed where he was, which only made Garvin more anxious.

"Then why?" He refused to touch his lips, even though they still tingled.

"Because at some point I developed feelings for you, and I thought that maybe you might feel the same way once you had a chance to grieve and heal. But you never did. You grieved and stayed stuck in that mode for so long." William leaned closer once again, which raised Garvin's temperature. "And then you fucking left, and I've been trying to figure out what to do about you ever since. So I came up here to see you again."

"And make a pass?" Garvin snapped.

William actually smiled. "No. I figured you and I could talk and maybe I could think some things through and get over you. But then here you are, and I see your deep blue eyes and the way your hair sticks up in the back and wants to fall into your eyes when you lean forward.

I remember John brushing it away, and I want to be the one to do that. I was never jealous of John. The kind of love you two had was amazingly special, and I guess I wanted it too."

Garvin tried to process what William was telling him, but his head refused. This was the last thing he'd expected. William was handsome and always had been, with his blond hair that shone in the sun and a face that with one look could make you do just about anything. No wonder William was always in demand as a model. He could sell sand to a man dying of thirst in the desert. "And you thought kissing me was going to do what?"

"Words are cheap. I figured actions would speak a lot louder. It's time you got back to the land of the living, and I wanted you to know that I hoped you could do that with me." William seemed almost lost. "I guess I was just being my usual stupid self."

"You've never been stupid," Garvin said. "But how am I supposed to process all this? I wasn't expecting to see you, and now I'm supposed to just deal with you being in love with me?"

William snickered. "And people think I'm the dumb one. I didn't say I was in love with you, though I probably could be. I'm saying that I have feelings for you. I don't know what they are, and I knew I never would unless I found you and tried to work it out."

Now William was starting to really confuse him.

"So you're not in love with me?" Garvin squirmed in his chair, his head spinning wildly.

"Weren't you listening? I don't know. The last time I fell in love...." The pain in William's eyes echoed what Garvin had felt for years after losing John. "You know how that ended."

"Ambrose was a complete jackass and a gold digger. I know you cared for him, but he didn't give a rat's ass for you. But that isn't your fault. Ambrose used you to try to advance his... thing... as some kind of social media influencer." Garvin remembered the turmoil, though he had been preoccupied at the time and still hip-deep in his own grief. Still, he knew he'd been there for William because that was what friends did.

"Yeah. It never felt like that," William said as he sat back in his chair. Sasha went over to him and placed his head on William's lap. "I always thought I wasn't good enough or didn't deserve to be happy."

Garvin leaned to the side as William stroked Sasha's head. "Look, Sasha sure seems to like you, and dogs have pure hearts, better than any of us. They know a good person." He took a deep breath. "Maybe both of us have to try to let some things go." He wasn't sure how he could do that, but William made him see that he had to try. He had been holding on to his grief and his pain for so long that maybe he didn't have anything else left. Maybe he didn't know how to feel unless he had them.

William smiled. "See, aren't you glad I came? You made a breakthrough."

Garvin covered his mouth and coughed. "You really are a screwed-up pain in the butt." Still, he couldn't help smiling.

"It takes one to know one," William retorted before getting up from his chair and wandering over to the window. "It seems like it's really late with how dark it is."

"You get used to it. Though I am ready for spring and summer. Then it's light all the time, so we sleep now and stay awake most of the summer." He winked, and William shook his head at the joke. "Still, it's only a little after eight." Leave it to William to show up on his doorstep—or in this case, nearly freeze to death and collapse in his carport—without any idea of what he was going to do. To make matters worse, he seemed to think he was in love with him. No matter what William said, you didn't kiss someone else like that without feeling something.

God, what the hell was Garvin going to do? First thing in the morning he needed to find out what happened to William's car and if it was even drivable. Then he was going to have to make sure William got back to Anchorage so he could go home. No matter how amazing that kiss had been, Garvin wasn't prepared to have William work his way into his life. The guy was the poster boy for not thinking any further ahead than his nose, and Garvin needed more than that. He needed to know what came next. It was how he'd made it through these years of loneliness after losing John.

"It feels so much later." William stood with his hands behind his back, rocking slightly from his toes to his heels. Garvin knew that movement meant William had something he was holding on to and wasn't ready to talk about. One thing about William—he had no poker face. Still, Garvin figured he'd talk about what was on his mind when he was ready. Sasha joined William at the window, nudging his hands for pets, which he of course got. The dog could be a pest when he wanted attention he wasn't getting. "What do you do to pass the time?" He didn't look away from the window as the aurora grew brighter and more intense, filling a good deal of the northern half of the night sky. "Is there television?"

"Not here. I don't really care for it. If I feel the need, I go down to the trading post. They have satellite and can get just about anything when the weather isn't too bad. I do have internet, so if I really want to watch something, I can go online, but I don't subscribe to a bunch of services."

William turned to him, his mouth hanging open. "What about *Real Housewives*? *The Kardashians*?"

Garvin was about to laugh, but the intensity of William's expression told him William was serious.

"How can you survive? I figured that even out here in the wilds of Alaska there would be some vestiges of…."

"Mind-numbing inanity?" Garvin joined him at the window. "Look out there. What do you see? That snow is two or three feet deep, and the lake is frozen nearly to the bottom in most places. It's almost twenty-five degrees below zero, and I only have so much propane to last me through the winter. In the summer and fall, I cut a ton of wood from the acreage away from the lake, split it, and use it to heat the place during much of the winter. I fish in the summer, and I hunt moose and other game, which is a lot of what I eat." He leaned forward. "Do you see the other house with lights on? That's Joe and Marie. Joe has a share of a fish wheel that catches salmon. He gets more than he can use, so I buy the fish he doesn't need and then process it into cans. It's a real late-summer and early-fall production at their house to get everything put up quickly."

"But you hate fish," William said.

"Yeah, I used to. Now it's a big part of my diet. I have a garden out back where I grow as many vegetables as I can here. Lots of potatoes and cool-climate greens. I have learned to do without tomatoes for the most part."

"It sounds like hell," William grumped.

"It's actually pretty wonderful. I know everyone who lives within thirty miles or so. We help each other out. Last fall I got a huge bull moose. Joe helped me butcher it, and Alan—his place is across the lake— he's mounting the head for me because it was worthy, in his words. I shared my bounty with a few others and was given bear and caribou in return. My freezers are full enough to last me through the winter, and for the things I need to buy, I teach school. I have a full life on my own, so I don't need to watch someone else's put-on, drama'd-up existence that's edited and hyped for maximum eye-rolling effect."

William seemed like he was in shock. "But...."

"Life here is hard. You should know that by now." Garvin turned to William, all teasing aside. "If you had been out there for another half hour, you could have lost your feet or hands to frostbite. Another hour and you would probably have frozen to death." Saying that sent a cold chill racing through him, because he knew in that moment that he did care and that it would have been a real loss. Fucking hell, that would have hurt. "This land up here isn't something to be taken lightly."

"I guess not." Garvin blinked hard as William continued watching him. "I really could have died," he whispered.

"Yes." And the best thing to do was to get William back to the city and on his way to someplace warmer where he wasn't going to get himself hurt... or worse. "You don't have the gear to stay up here." Garvin figured if he scared him a little and explained that he didn't have what it took to be here, William wouldn't argue about going back.

"Then is there a place where I can get the things I need? Obviously better boots, and a heavier coat and snow pants. Maybe your friends at this trading post can help me. I'm sure they sell stuff like that. You can take me over there tomorrow. I've got my credit cards and money. I took those with me when I left the car. The keys too. They're in the inner coat pocket. I wasn't going to leave that stuff to be stolen."

Garvin sighed. "You want to stay? After everything you've been through?"

"Of course. I did come all this way and almost die." The way William looked at him made all of the arguments against staying slip from Garvin's mind. There were times when William was the most exasperating person on earth. "Besides, I wanted to see you again." And just like he always did, he slipped past Garvin's defenses, leaving him without an argument.

"If you're sure."

"Yeah. Besides…." William licked his perfect lips. "I know you'd never let anything happen to me."

Fuck, what was he supposed to do with that? As Garvin tried to figure this shit out, William wandered through the main room of the cabin. "You know, this place is kind of cute. It needs a few things to make it more homey, though. I mean, you could use some curtains and stuff. It would help make the place warmer and more cozy." He put his hands on his hips and turned in a slow circle. "The moose head will look great over on that wall. The rustic wood is really nice, and there's even a hole already, so you won't have to make another one. That's really good." He seemed to be exploring Garvin's small living space. "So where are the bedrooms?"

"Mine is through there, and that's the bathroom. I leave the doors open so the heat can circulate." The entire place was less than eight hundred square feet, and Garvin liked it that way. "I'll get you some blankets for the sofa, and you can sleep there."

William continued wandering, peeking into Garvin's room as well as the bathroom before returning to the living area. He said nothing, and Garvin wondered what was going on in that head of his. "If that's what you want."

"Excuse me?" Garvin asked as William glided up to him in that way he had. Sometimes William seemed to half float when he moved. He was always so damned graceful and, if Garvin was honest, sexy as all hell.

"Well, there's one bedroom and a bed big enough for the two of us." He stood right in front of Garvin, and before he could say anything, William's hands glided along his cheek, warm and soft, his caress gentle, and yet intense enough to make him shiver. "Isn't it best when it's cold if we share bodily warmth? I've wanted to do that for a long time, and I did come all this way."

Garvin snorted. "That has to be the cheesiest line I have ever heard in my life."

William rolled his eyes and then held Garvin's gaze. "It isn't a line. You and I used to go out together, remember? I have never used a line on anyone, and I have never needed to." That was for fucking sure. Guys swarmed up to William like he had been dipped in testosterone and they were all on hormone replacement therapy.

Garvin swallowed hard, because he had seen what William had under his clothes when they went to the gym together. He was a gay man, so he looked, and there was no doubting that William was in tip-top prime shape. But being in the same bed with him was not a good idea. The two of them together was a recipe for disaster. Not that he didn't think that William could control himself; that wasn't the issue. It was the other way around. "That isn't a good idea, and you know it."

William chuckled softly. "Are you kidding? I think it's one of the best ideas I have ever had." He closed the distance between them. "I know you think I have fluff between my ears and that I don't pay attention to stuff around me, but I do... well, sometimes, if it's important to me."

Garvin bit back the snarky comment that threatened. "O-kay...."

"Hey. I can hear the way you're breathing." He put his hand in the center of Garvin's chest. "Your heart is beating like a drum, fast, and your eyes are wide and dilated. I know what that means. You can say anything you want, but I know you feel something for me and that you're scared. It's been a long time since John died, though, and you deserve to move on."

"I did. I sold everything and came up here."

William snickered. "You just changed from a studio to a location shoot." Whatever the hell that meant. "You're still doing the same thing. You hide yourself away. You did it in West Hollywood, and now you're doing it here." He shrugged again. "Fine. Look, I promise to be a gentleman and not make a pass at you." He turned to the sofa. "That thing isn't long enough for either of us to sleep on. So I'll be good... I promise."

Garvin could not believe he was contemplating this. "Fine. But you have to sleep on Sasha's side of the bed, and he snores and sometimes runs in his sleep. Under normal circumstances he's a bed hog, so don't be surprised if you end up on the floor." Garvin smiled at the shock on William's face.

"Doesn't he have a bed of his own?" William asked. "Fine. I can share with Sasha here. I'm sure he's a very good dog." He was still nervous, and Garvin wondered just what he was getting himself into. William knelt down, and Sasha went right up to him. "You need to leave me some room in the bed. Okay?"

"Don't count on it," Garvin said, and then William shifted his gaze, and Garvin wondered if he was the one who should be concerned. He could keep his hands to himself. The real issue was if he truly wanted to.

CHAPTER 4

BEFORE BED, Garvin made a snack of some crackers and cheese. William wasn't too hungry, but he nibbled a little. "You need to eat. Up here, the cold has a way of catching up with you, and after what happened this afternoon, your body is going to need the calories to heal." Garvin also gave him a glass of juice that he gulped down quickly.

"It's so dry here. I didn't expect that." William sat back down.

"Cold air doesn't hold moisture. There's no room. So it snows and then becomes very dry. I'm told that if it's cold enough and you throw a mug of hot coffee in the air, nothing will come down. It will vaporize instantly because of how dry it is."

William kept finding himself wandering nervously to the window to look at the light show and then to the kitchen area again before going back to the window. Maybe Garvin was right. He hadn't actually said it, but his tone carried more than enough rebuke. Maybe this was the stupidest idea he had ever had… and goodness knows he'd had more than his share of doozies. How he got himself into these situations was beyond him. William knew he wasn't a bad person, and he never set out to do the wrong thing—it just seemed to happen to him. His grandmother always told him that he was a "leap before you look" kind of guy. That sort of decision-making seemed to work for him, at least as far as his career was concerned.

Most people knew it was a long shot to break into show business in any way. It took talent and a great deal of luck. William knew that now, but at the time he was starting, he just figured he had what it took and that doors should open for him… and they did. That was the amazing thing. Maybe they shouldn't have, because William hadn't struggled. Everything just fell into place. Maybe he expected that everything else would do that. Even though he knew he was lucky, part of him still thought he was some sort of golden boy.

"Have you ever tried the coffee thing?" William asked, pulling his mind out of thoughts of himself. His mind always went there.

"No. It doesn't get that cold here, but it does farther north," Garvin said. He added more wood to the fire and closed the stove door. William tried to stifle a yawn, but fatigue was quickly catching up with him. "Let me get you something to sleep in." Garvin trudged off with Sasha right behind him.

William once again looked out the window. The aurora still lit up the sky, and he wondered at the beauty of this place. He could see how it could entice you. It had lured William into coming up here and then getting out of the car. Maybe this was the stupidest thing he had ever done in his life, and he should go back to the city and the warmth and let Garvin go on with his life.

With his host out of the room, William took a closer look around. The walls held a few pictures. A taxidermied squirrel sat on a shelf, and there were a few photos, mostly Garvin with people William didn't know. One thing that jumped out at him was that there were no pictures of John, William, or anyone from back in California. Even on the simple bookshelves in the corner, there were just books and a few knickknacks that might have been in the cabin since it was built. But there was little of Garvin or, particularly, his earlier life.

"You can use these," Garvin said from behind him.

"Thanks." William took the clothes and used the bathroom to get into the sweatpants and T-shirt. He also cleaned up a little before joining Garvin in the bedroom.

The truth was he was a little nervous. Garvin was already under the covers, and Sasha lay curled up on the other half of the bed. "That's enough. You need to give William room."

The dog huffed and jumped down. William climbed in the other side and pulled up the thick covers, waiting for the warmth to build.

"I'll probably get up a few times in the night to add wood to the fire. I usually do. The heat will kick on if it gets too cold in here."

"Thanks, Garvin." William rolled over. "For everything." He closed his eyes as Sasha jumped back onto the bed and walked over near his feet before thudding down on top of them. "Your dog is trying to squish my feet." He bumped his feet upward, determined the dog wasn't going to beat him for bed space. Sasha growled when William moved his feet higher. "Stop it, you giant ball of hair. I'm way more diva than you are." He pushed harder, and Sasha shifted over.

"Well played," Garvin said. "Now go to sleep and get some rest. You need it." His voice was cool, but then he lightly stroked William's shoulder under the covers. "We'll deal with everything in the morning."

Exhaustion caught up with him in minutes, and William went right to sleep.

IT WAS still dark when he woke again. Sasha had worked his way upward, pressing William right next to Garvin, who had an arm around his waist. They were almost spooned together. The important thing was that William was warm. He shifted slightly, and two things became immediately apparent. The first was that something thick, long, and very hard pressed against his butt, and the other was that Garvin's hand was an inch away from his own excitement, which throbbed when he thought of Garvin's cock pressed to him. William considered rolling over and making the most of this development, but no. He lay still, deciding it was best to ignore the situation. Then Garvin nestled closer, and that became impossible.

William stifled a groan and tried to close his eyes, but all his attention centered on certain pieces of his anatomy that seemed to have a mind of their own. Garvin had made it pretty clear that he wasn't interested in William, at least not sexually or in any way other than William being his pain-in-the-neck friend. Besides, Garvin was asleep, and things like that happened. It didn't mean anything.

Sasha stood up and jumped to the floor. William slowly slipped away from Garvin and then got up. It was still dark, even though the clock read after seven in the morning. He stepped on the floor and did his best not to groan at the cold. The furnace was running, so at least the house was minimally warm. William used the bathroom and found his socks, which he pulled on before going to the living room.

The stove had nearly gone out, but William put in some of the smaller prices of wood. They caught, and he added some larger logs and closed the door to let the stove heat up. Sasha stood by the door.

"I suppose you want me to let you out." William was almost afraid to check the temperature. He cracked the door just wide enough for Sasha to get through and then closed it again, shivering at the frigid air. William wondered if he should wait, but a scratch told him Sasha was back, and he hurried right inside again.

"Thank you for letting him out," Garvin said as he came out of the bedroom. "And for starting the fire." He was already dressed and even had his hair combed. "I need to get online and get my students started for the morning," he explained as he poured two mugs of coffee and brought one to William. "Did you sleep okay?"

"Like a log. I guess I was tired, though I did wake up to something poking me." William figured he'd jab the bear to see if he got a reaction.

"Sasha does that sometimes." Garvin put another log on the fire and closed the stove door.

William cleared his throat. "Somehow I don't think it was Sasha." He couldn't keep his mouth shut.

Garvin hesitated for only a moment before going to sit in the corner of the room at a desk in front of the bookshelves. He started his computer and, after a few seconds, peered around the side of the screen. William pretended not to see him and sat on the sofa, pulling a blanket over his legs. Sasha jumped up and settled next to him. It seemed William had made his first doggie friend, and he stroked Sasha's thick fur, watching Garvin for a few minutes before getting something to read to pass the time.

"ARE YOU done?" William asked, stretching. He'd dozed off with his book. It was nearly one in the afternoon, and his belly was starting to eat itself. Normally William had a minimal appetite, but not today.

"Yes. The lessons are done, and the homework assignments are already starting to come in. I've corrected those and sent them right back. I'll have to work again this afternoon to finish grading their assignments. I also called the trooper in this area about your car. It was towed out, and they brought it to the trading post. One of the guys will get it running for you. Enrique said that there didn't seem to be any body damage."

"I see. That's good." Last night William had been so confident about Garvin and staying, but maybe he should just drive back to Anchorage and get a flight home. "I don't know what to say. That was very nice."

"Everyone helps out here. Let's get you dressed properly and we'll head out." Garvin got him a heavier coat and other snow gear. They were a little big on him, but he put on a few other layers to fill out with some bulk. Garvin banked the fire and checked that William was all set. Sasha sat by the door, bounding out as soon as Garvin opened the door to a frigid winter postcard. Snow drifted down from everywhere, covering everything. The gray clouds hung low over the lake. The light was even more muted than yesterday, and it felt like it was late in the day rather than the middle of it.

"You want me to ride on that?" William asked, taking the helmet Garvin handed him before jumping onto the snowmobile.

"Yes. Now get on. It's the best way to get around this time of year." He started the engine, and William got on behind Garvin, slipping his hands around his waist. Something like this should have been a dream, but as soon as Garvin started forward, William held on tighter and prayed he didn't die or freeze to death.

Neither happened, and after a few minutes, William relaxed a little. Though occasionally cold air found its way in, he was still warmer than he had been traipsing through the woods. To stay warm, he pressed closer to Garvin and used him as a windbreak. It was nice being this close to him. They slowed when they reached the highway, and then continued onward before pulling up in front of a rustic but sturdy building. William didn't know quite what to make of it, but the inside was warm, and that was the most important thing. He hung up his gear next to Garvin's and took a few seconds to look around.

"Guys, this is William, a friend from a previous life in LA. It was his car that was stranded." Garvin motioned William to a small table, and William sat down, grateful that Garvin hadn't highlighted his stupidity.

A huge man slipped off his stool. "I'm Big Bob, and I'll look at your car for you to make sure it starts. We found your gear in the back seat, and Enrique brought it inside for you."

"Thanks. I appreciate that. I intended to surprise Garvin with a visit, but I guess we both got more than I bargained for." He shrugged, and Bob clapped him on the back.

"I don't doubt it. This is the Alaskan bush, and plenty of folks get more than they were counting on out here." He laughed. "Just be glad you made it in one piece."

"Thanks. I'm glad I'm here." He glanced around again and then sat down. This really did seem like a totally different world. Guys sat at the bar with beards that hadn't been trimmed in days, or maybe ever. Guys back home made sure everything was perfect before they stepped out the door, and here, these men were just as God made them… so to speak.

"The menu is on the board. It's pretty basic, but everything is good."

"Why don't you order for me." He rubbed his hands together. "And I'm going to do what I do best: shopping." He spotted racks of winter gear and figured he would make sure he stayed warm. He wandered over and began looking through what they had.

"You seem like a fish out of water," a handsome man said, and William wondered where he'd seen him before.

"I am a little." He held out his hand. "William. I'm visiting from LA, and I need proper gear. I borrowed what I'm wearing from Garvin, and as you can see, it's a little big." They shook hands.

"Devon."

William gasped. "You're the artist." He grinned as Devon nodded. "I knew I recognized you. I saw you at your show in Hollywood last year. Your work is amazing. I bought one of the pieces and have it hanging in my condo. It's my favorite of all time." He restrained himself from going complete fanboy all over the place. Still, he pulled out his phone to show Devon the work he had and where he had placed it.

"That scene is from this side of the lake, less than a mile from here. It's near the library." Devon seemed pleased.

"I think I read you live here."

Devon smiled. "My husband owns the trading post. He's working in the back right now. And you're visiting Garvin." He looked at William strangely.

"We're old friends," William said.

"I see." Devon had one of those gazes that left him wondering just how deeply he was looking. It was almost unsettling. "I'm glad Garvin has some company. He spends a lot of his time alone. We tried fixing him up with a friend…."

William wanted to growl. He had no right to be possessive of Garvin, but he felt it anyway. Devon nodded, and William wondered how much his expression had given away.

"But he's a tough nut to crack."

William snickered. "I'm good with that." He glanced at Garvin, who was talking to a couple of guys. Their gazes met for a second, and William swallowed at the momentary heat that flared and then slipped away.

Devon seemed to understand. "You'll have to be. I attempted to paint Garvin last summer. He was sitting outside his cabin by the lake. I rowed across and sat in the boat, looking and drawing."

"Did he get upset?"

Devon shook his head. "It wasn't that. As I watched him, he looked up, and my hands stopped midstroke. His eyes were filled with pain and loneliness. It hit me hard, and before I knew it, I had drawn him that way. I still have it, but I can't bring myself to paint him, because every time I look closely enough, it's all I see."

William wiped his eyes as laughter filled the room. Garvin sat next to the other guys, who had all shared something funny, and there it was, those brooding eyes. Garvin's lips had turned upward and he was laughing with the rest, but it didn't reach that far.

"You see it too," Devon said, and he nodded. William had to admit that until this moment he hadn't, but as soon as Devon mentioned it, William wondered how he could have missed it all this time.

"Yeah, I do now, and I know the source of it." He wasn't going to talk about Garvin's past. That wasn't his information to share. "But I don't know if there's anything I can do to help." Or if Garvin would ever let him, or anyone, in again.

"Will you try?" Devon asked.

William nodded. "I'll do my best." It seemed that maybe what he wanted and what might be best for Garvin lined up. At least that was what Garvin's friends thought. But with Garvin, the hard part was getting him to unclench long enough for anyone to make it past his sphincter-tight defenses. "But if I'm going to stay, I'm going to need proper winter gear that will fit me."

"I can help with that. But don't expect anything to be very fashionable."

As cold as it was outside, fashion was the last thing William was worried about. Devon helped him find a dark coat and pants that actually fit and didn't look hideous, so William considered that a win. He also got some extra-heavy socks. The boots Garvin had loaned him fit well, so he was lucky there. None of the ones at the trading post fit. By the time he was done, he'd racked up quite a bill. He handed Devon his credit card and joined Garvin at the table.

"Get everything?" Garvin asked as their lunch was brought.

William nodded, his mouth watering. He thanked Angie and dug into the cut of meat with gusto. He was pretty sure it wasn't beef but didn't ask. It tasted good—slightly earthy, but he was hungry enough to eat a bear... even if he hoped he actually wasn't.

CHAPTER 5

"WHAT WERE you and Devon talking about?" Garvin asked once William paused in his eating. William was usually a fastidious eater, so to have him practically shoveling in his food meant he must really be hungry.

He swallowed. "His art. I have one of his pieces, and he said it was the view from over by the library. It's my favorite. I guess I knew he lived up here. But I never made the connection until a few minutes ago." He cut off another piece of his small venison steak. Blacktail deer were common throughout the state, and Enrique must have gotten one in recently.

"That's cool. I see he got you some winter gear. Does that mean you'll be staying longer?" Part of him wanted William to stay, and another part—the one built of years of habit and keeping himself locked away—wanted something else.

"I came all this way, and...." He set down his fork. "Dang, that's good. A little peppery, but tender."

"It's venison," Garvin told him.

"Cool. I had that growing up plenty of times." William came from a small town in the upper part of Michigan. Garvin should have known that venison and other game would be familiar to him. "I wish my dad had cooked it like this." He picked up his fork once more. "Look, if you want me to go, then I'll wait until Bob gets the car running and go. I'm not going to stay where I'm not wanted." He leaned forward. "So my staying is up to you." He went back to eating, and Garvin sat back.

This was the moment when he had to decide what he wanted, at least as far as William's visit was concerned. "Then if you want to, you should stay." He didn't want to tell William to go because… well, it was nice having someone around, and he liked William. Sleeping with him last night had been difficult. Honestly, it had been more than that. All night long he'd listened to William's soft breathing, and more than once, his scent had filled Garvin's nose, driving him crazy. And yeah, he had to admit that it was difficult trying to go to sleep when his dick throbbed in his sleep pants and there was nothing he could do about it. Having William right there, knowing he was so close and yet keeping to himself, was going to be an exercise in self-control. But having William leave....

"Are you sure?" William asked.

Garvin nodded. "We can contact the rental company to send someone up to get the car."

"That's really something," William said as he went over to watch the snow. "I haven't seen anything like that since I was a kid. We used to get storms that would come through, and I'd look out the front window and everything would be white." Garvin stood next to him.

"I'm going to get your car running before the weather gets too bad." Bob looked huge all bundled up. He went outside, and Garvin shivered just thinking about it.

"How long do you think it will be?" William asked.

"Bob told me he got the block heater running on the car a while ago, so with any luck it won't be too long." Garvin figured he'd go on out and see if he could give Bob a hand just as he came back inside.

"You're good to go. She started right back up. Only problem seems to be that the battery got jolted and it wouldn't hold a charge. It just needed a chance to warm up a little and go back to normal. Plug in the block heater once you get to Garvin's and you should be fine. I brought the suitcases inside to protect them from the cold just in case."

"Thank you so much for everything." William began pulling on the gear he'd worn over. Devon came out with a pair of bags, and once Garvin had his gear on, he placed them in the trunk.

"Would you mind taking Sasha with you?" Garvin asked as William put his purchases on the seat.

"Sure. Come on, Sasha, get inside," he called, and the dog jumped right in back. "I'll follow you to the cabin." William got into the sedan.

Probably the worst kind of vehicle for weather like this—it was so light. No wonder William went off the road. Still, Garvin got on the snowmobile and led the way back to the cabin, taking his time and making sure William was okay.

By the time they arrived, the wind was howling, blowing snow everywhere. Garvin had William cut the engine and then got his car plugged in. Garvin let Sasha inside, and then he and William carried everything into the cabin and closed the door. "I need to bring in some more wood. We're going to need it against this kind of weather."

"I'll get the fire started," William told him, and Garvin went back out into the storm to grab an armful of logs from under the carport. He set it by the door and went for a second load, then a third, before finally going inside, where he stripped off his outer layer.

The fire was already going, and William picked the wood up off the floor and put it in the box before closing the lid. William stripped off his outer gear, and Garvin hung it all up. "Where do you want me to put my stuff?"

"In my bedroom. There's a chest along the far wall. You can use it to put your bags on, and your gear you bought can be hung by the door." While William got situated, Garvin got a pot of coffee going before settling in to grade the last of his papers so he could return them to the kids. He needed to make the most of it in case the power went out.

"So, what do you do out here for fun?" William asked when he came out in heavy sweats and a bulky sweater. "Let me guess, there's another trading post of sorts twenty miles up the road, and you all pile in trucks and go up there for kicks."

"Smartass… and the next place is fifty miles north, or you can go into Palmer or Wasilla. As for fun… well, most of the people out here expend much of their effort ensuring they can survive." He poured William some coffee and carried it over to him. "This is a very different life from the one you lead in LA. Out here we're closer to nature. We don't fight her or try to bend her to our will. Instead we live with her… more or less."

"Really?"

Garvin nodded. "I hunt quite a bit, but my skill tends more toward fishing. I got a bear last year, and my friend Joe helped me butcher it and then prepare the meat properly. It can be very tough, so he showed me how to marinate it and the way to cook it so it both tastes good and gets tender. I told you about my moose. I also hunted caribou and deer, as well as small game. But like I said, mostly I fish in season. The wood we're burning I cut myself. The property goes back quite a ways, and I cut down only selected trees. The rest I let grow."

William slowly sipped his coffee. "And this is the kind of life that you want? You like it here?"

Garvin hesitated and wished he hadn't. "I like it. My life is much simpler than it was... before. There aren't complex motivations, and I understand all the people around me. Bob is a great guy, and he can fix anything with an engine. He keeps all the equipment running for everyone for miles around. Enrique is a born host. He makes sure that we have what we need, and he can get almost anything we want. All we have to do is tell him. Devon... well, he paints, and he makes Enrique happy. He will also lend a hand to anyone who needs it. Last summer he heard I was cutting wood and stopped over just to help out. And me... well, I keep all the computers and electronics running and up to date. If someone has a problem, they let Enrique know, and he tells me. I meet them at the trading post so I can fix it." He shrugged. There was nothing complex or hidden out here. That was part of why Garvin liked it. He'd had enough of complex situations and hidden agendas to last a lifetime.

"I get that everyone works together. I suppose it's a small community up here, especially during the winter." William slid closer on the sofa, his earthy scent driving him a little crazy.

After John died, Garvin had been a complete mess. He hadn't wanted to leave the house for weeks after the funeral. Groceries had been delivered, and he'd stayed at home. He'd withdrawn from everyone and everything. After all, life hadn't been fair in the least. John had been an amazing man—gifted, generous, caring, strong.... He'd also been impatient, and that had driven him all his life. Anyway... after those months of reclusiveness, it had been William who had forced his way in and practically dragged Garvin out for dinner with a group of friends. Garvin hadn't been ready, but then he probably never would have been.

"But is that the reason you stay?" William's question cut through his thoughts.

"What?"

William sat back, his blue eyes watching intensely. "I've known you for a long time. John died almost seven years ago. It took a long time before you rejoined the living, and when you did, it was like you would rather cut everyone off."

Garvin sighed. "As I remember, you wouldn't let me." He wanted to be snarky about it but couldn't. He knew his friends cared, but he hadn't been able to bring himself to be concerned with anything back then. Did that make him as asshole? Probably.

"Is that why you moved out here? You could be alone and withdrawn and no one was going to care?" He sipped the coffee, and for someone who could be so clueless at times, especially about the consequences of his own actions, William sure hit the nail on the head with that one. "Rather than be a part of your own life again—and those of the people who care about you—you just gave up, moved up here, and could spend the rest of your life alone, wallowing in your sea of self-pity."

"Hey," Garvin snapped. "It's my life, and if I want to be alone, then that's my decision."

William leaned closer, his eyes flecked with purple, his gaze growing harder as the wind whipped around the cabin, sending a chill through Garvin. "But what you really want is to have John back, and you can't. He isn't coming back, no matter how long you stay by yourself trying to tell the gods that you're miserable, or something. They don't care, and you can't have John back. It doesn't work that way."

"I know that," he said firmly. "God knows I have wished to have more time with him ever since the day he died right in front of me." Sometimes that day seemed like yesterday, and he was right back there in the pain and confusion, losing the one person he thought he would be able to rely on for the rest of his life.

"Do you? Or are you just stuck?" William asked.

Garvin stood up because he needed to move away from William. "You think you get to come up here, sit on my sofa, and tell me what I'm doing wrong?"

Damn it all, William stayed where he was and seemed calm. "Someone has to." He drank some more and set the mug on the table. "I know you miss John, but it's been a long time. Do you remember what it was like to live with him? What John loved most other than you? Can you remember how he smelled or what he looked like? Or are you grieving and wishing he was here out of habit, or just because you think it's what you have to do?" Garvin thought he was going to explode as William got to his feet. "John was a wonderful friend, the best. He also went, like, a million miles an hour all the time. Do you remember how he could barely sit through dinner? His legs would shake because he had so much energy. His mind went as fast as the rest of him. He threw all he had into everything he did, starting the business, building it into the online powerhouse it still is today… loving you." William looked hurt. "We all miss him. That spirit he had that infected everyone around him."

Garvin's shoulders slumped. "He swept me off my feet after two dates," he remembered. "The two of us struggled together for the first few years, but then John finished medical school. He was a brilliant doctor, an amazing businessman. The practice started off slow at first, but he had a vision. He worked night and day for months to get it off the ground, and once others saw how he did business, they wanted to work with him and the practice grew even more. And yet he always found time for me." He swallowed hard. "John worked hard, but even when we were in school and had just met, he never canceled a date or showed up late. He supported me when I went into teaching." Garvin was tearing up.

"John was so proud of you," William said, and Garvin nodded.

"I made peanuts compared to him, and yet he always told me that what I did was more important. He never missed a function at school." Garvin stared at the near whiteout conditions. "I remember the time he had flown to Tokyo for a huge medical conference that he was supposed to speak at. My kids had a concert that night, and I knew he would miss it. I went to school, helped set up, and got the kids all in place. When we all stepped out on stage, there was John in the second row. I'd never seen him look so happy or so tired, but he clapped and cheered for all the kids, and then the next day, he flew back to Tokyo to speak and bring the international medical conference to a close." Garvin wiped his eyes. "I always knew where I stood with him because John made sure I—"

"John always made you feel like you were the most important thing in his world," William said.

Garvin nodded. "Do you know what it's like to have that and then have it ripped away? To know what true happiness is, and then have it come to an end in your arms?" He shivered and barely noticed as William added more wood to the fire.

"I can't say I do." William closed the stove door. "But I know that John would not like this. He wanted you to be happy. John wanted both of you to be happy, and I just think that would mean you rejoining the land of the living."

Garvin turned around. "And I suppose that means going back to LA?" That was never going to happen. His life there was over, and going back wasn't an option.

"I didn't mean that. But you need to find a way to be happy. To stop living like you expect John to walk thorough your door at any moment and you're just waiting for that to happen." William kept his voice low.

Garvin didn't know how to respond, because at some level he knew that William might very well be right. "How in the hell do you know how I feel?" he snapped.

"Because I miss him too. John wasn't my husband, and we were never lovers, but he was there for me too. You know that John and I knew each other before he met you and that we met in college. It was John who pushed me to go to my first audition. He drove me there and waited outside until I was done. Then he drove me to the next one. I wasn't going to go because I didn't feel well, but he practically manhandled me into the car. I got that job—and the one after it—because of him."

All of a sudden, Garvin could see what William was doing as he stood by the stove, soaking up the heat. He was channeling John. No wonder William seemed different than he usually did. "And now you think you need to return the favor?"

"No. But maybe it's time you came out of your shell and just let yourself live again." William crossed the room and stood right next to him. "God knows I'm not John and can't replace him, but…."

Garvin had had enough of this conversation. When he'd asked William to stay, he hadn't expected a dissection of his entire life to be part of the deal. "How about we let this go. I promise I'll try to… I don't know… get out there and try to live a little more, if you promise not to bring this up for the rest of your visit. Okay? We can just be…."

He almost said *friends*, but the word stuck in his throat. William looked stunning in the waning daylight, and as much as he wanted to discount his own feelings, having William here made him happy.

"Okay," William said. If Garvin expected them to shake hands, what he got was a hug that left him breathless and his body on fire, hotter than the flames in the stove. Damn it all, he shouldn't feel this way, but William's hard body against him and the way he seemed so strong and permanent had a wave of excitement running through him. And damned if he didn't feel that same excitement pressed against him.

Garvin backed away. "I should see about dinner." It was early, but he needed to do something to back away from William and this attraction he knew he shouldn't feel… and yet he couldn't help wanting him so damned bad.

CHAPTER 6

WILLIAM KNEW something wasn't right—tension washed off Garvin—but he wasn't sure he should ask him about it. They had talked about some pretty intense subjects, and maybe it was too much for him. William probably should have kept his mouth shut. Talking too damned much had always been one of his flaws, and while what he'd said had been what he felt, it was pretty obvious that Garvin didn't agree.

Maybe William was stupid to think that he would agree. Garvin had been spiraling for years. William smiled as he thought about that term. He'd heard it in a TV show and never understood it until now. "Garvin... are you going to be okay?" He went to where he was making dinner at the small counter and stood across from him. "I didn't mean to hurt your feelings."

"You didn't," Garvin said without looking up. "I'm just trying to work through some things." He continued working.

"Okay. But why are you chopping the poor onion to near oblivion?"

Garvin's knife came to a stop. "Shit." The poor thing was nearly paste.

William blinked his watering eyes as Garvin slid the mush on the cutting board into the trash. William watched and waited, hoping Garvin would open up. It usually worked pretty well. Or it used to. He'd had to learn patience over the years. It was not something that came easily to him.

"What am I supposed to do?" Garvin finally asked as he began cutting a new onion. "You're here, and we're going to be in this cabin for a couple days. The road is going to be blown shut, and the snow will be a couple feet deep by the time this ends. We can go in on the snowmobile, but that's about it."

"And that makes you nervous?"

Garvin shook his head. "You do."

"I make you nervous." He leaned over the counter. "How do I do that?" It was too much to expect that the nerves came from the same source as his own.

Garvin shrugged. "It's probably just me. I need to learn not to overthink every single thing in my life." He finished the onion and then began cutting four slices of bacon. He added that to a pan and got it cooking just as the lights switched off and the room went dark.

"Crap," Garvin swore. "Come over here and watch this. I need to get the lamps."

William took over browning the bacon while Garvin opened the end upper cabinet and set out some battery-operated lamps. They were bright enough to see pretty well by. Once there was light, Garvin took over the cooking once more. "I have more batteries, so we aren't going to have to worry about light. But the propane furnace isn't going to run because it needs power for the fan. So we have the stove for warmth."

"Do you need me to do anything?" William asked.

"Bundle up and bring in some more wood to fill the box. We have to make sure we have enough to get through the night. Sasha should also go out and do his business. But stay under the shelter of the carport and out of the wind." He continued cooking as William pulled on his gear before calling Sasha and opening the door.

As he stepped outside, the wind caught him. Damn, that was cold. He turned so his back was to it and managed to find the wood pile. It was dark as hell, snow swirling everywhere. Fortunately, Sasha took about three steps, peed, pooped, and hurried back to the door. William used the light from the window to guide him as he let the dog inside and followed with his load of wood. "God, it's something else." He filled the wood box and retrieved another load, adding what he could to the box before placing what was left on the floor next to it.

"You should have taken a light," Garvin said.

"I guess I'm so used to the city, where there's always light no matter what time it is." He hung up his gear and added more wood to the stove, building the heat, then closed the stove door. "What else do we do?"

"Wait out the storm. The power won't be back on until it's over, and things like this can last a couple of days. We have plenty of food and wood. We'll need to melt snow for water for everything, including the toilet, because the pump needs power, but from the looks of things, we'll have a ton of that."

"Do you need me to get some?"

Garvin shook his head. "I'll take care of that after dinner." He went back to cooking, and William nervously wandered around the small room. Every time the wind whistled outside, it sounded like it was trying to get in. "It's okay. This happens here, and I have everything we could need to wait it out. It happens a couple times a winter."

"How can you stand it all alone?" It was bad enough when Garvin was with him. But going through this alone was more than William could think about. "What do you do if, I don't know, a tree falls on the cabin or the wind sends something through a window?" His imagination was really going for it, and he was having a hard time reining it in. William hated that his chicken side was on display, but he couldn't stop it. He was literally in the middle of nowhere in a cabin that didn't even have power, and the only things standing between them and freezing to death were these walls and the fire. The more he thought about it, the more agitated he became.

"This cabin has been here for forty years, and the trees nearby are strong and sturdy. I know every single one of them in my woods, and those that are weaker are cut down for firewood or building material. Nothing out here goes to waste. Just relax and remember that it's only the wind."

"And a shit-ton of snow," William retorted, trying not to shiver as the wind howled once more. He would have liked it if Garvin had come over to comfort him with more than words, but he stayed in the kitchen. The scent of bacon and onions soon filled the space, adding a sense of warmth that William didn't know was possible. "I can't believe you remembered."

"That this is one of your favorites?" Garvin asked before adding the tomato and garlic, and maybe a touch of oregano. It was hard to tell in the light, but the familiar scent of Garvin's pasta sauce seemed to calm the wave of worry that threatened to take over. It wasn't long before they sat together on the sofa, blankets over their legs, eating the old favorite, simple pasta that always tasted like Garvin. No one made this the way he did—no one ever had—and William sat close enough to him that Garvin's heat warmed his leg.

"Thanks for this." He lightly bumped Garvin's shoulder as he wolfed down the food. Maybe it was the worry, or the simple fact that earlier in the day he had been out in the frigid air, but he was hungrier than he could ever remember. Usually he was so worried about his weight and how he looked that he never gave really good food much thought. It was to be avoided in order to preserve his image. But this… well. This was to be enjoyed, savored. As William turned, he knew its maker was supposed to be loved, because anyone who could put this kind of warmth and care into a bowl of pasta deserved more than living alone in a cabin. William wanted that for Garvin, and hell, he wanted to be that person.

He had already been in love with him, in a way, for quite some time. That wasn't the issue. William knew what his heart wanted. Hell, the damned thing pounded in his ears whenever Garvin was nearby. The real issue was how closed off Garvin was, and how William could get him to open up. That eluded him. William ate his pasta, hands shaking just because Garvin was next to him. There had to be something he could do.

GARVIN WAS right: the power stayed off and the cabin largely dark. They turned off many of the lanterns to save the batteries and sat in front of the fire. William stared into the flames, wondering what he was going to do with Garvin, and came to the conclusion that there wasn't much he *could* do. Garvin would either open his heart or not, and there was little William could do to pry open that particular black gate except make sure Garvin knew that he wasn't going to run on him, even though at the moment, he wanted nothing more than to get out of this frozen landscape, where every gust of wind sent a chill through him.

"We need to sleep," Garvin said. Sasha had curled himself in front of the fire, and William had the blanket up over him so only his head stuck out. He had no intention of moving to the other room no matter how comfortable that mattress was. It was too cold in there. Hell, it was just warm enough out here near the fire. "Get up, okay?"

William was skeptical, but he did as Garvin asked, keeping the blanket around him. Garvin went to the back of the sofa and fiddled with it until the back came down, making a flat space. "Oh."

"I've had to sleep out here near the fire before." He hurried away and returned with a couple of pillows and a few more blankets. He covered the cushion with a sheet before spreading out the blankets. "Go get cleaned up and leave the bathroom door open while I finish up here."

William didn't have to be told twice. He hurried to the bedroom, where he grabbed some night clothes and raced to the bathroom with some water they'd heated on the stove. Never in his life had he changed clothes or cleaned up so quickly. Leaving the door open as Garvin said, he returned to the room, where Garvin had everything set up. Sasha jumped up and tried to make himself comfortable in the middle.

"No. Get down," Garvin scolded, and Sasha slowly trudged off the bed and back onto the floor, looking at both of them like they were the Grinch and he was some kind of orphaned Who. "You can stay by the fire."

Garvin hurried off while William settled quickly under the covers, shivering until the blankets warmed. By the time Garvin returned, William had made this little cocoon, and he didn't dare move. "Keep your cold parts off me," William teased as Garvin got in on the other side.

"I thought friends shared," Garvin said as he scooched closer.

"God, your feet are like ice." William tried to move away, but there wasn't that much room.

"So are yours," Garvin retorted when William gave him a dose of his toes on his calf. He chuckled at the game as Garvin drew closer, sliding an arm over his hip and then around his belly. Finally William was starting to feel warm… and as soon as that happened, his dick stood up to take notice. William decided to ignore it. Clearly Garvin was going to, and there was no use making things weird between them. Well, weird*er*.

"There's enough wood?" William asked.

"Yes. Plenty. Just relax and go to sleep. Sasha is right there. I'm willing to bet that at some point in the night, he'll climb onto the bed, and that dog can put out heat like nothing else."

"Okay. But what about the fire?"

"I'll keep it going," Garvin said, and William settled back into the warmth.

He should have been able to go to sleep. He was warm and tired as hell. But every time he closed his eyes, his mind settled on where Garvin held him. William scooted closer to Garvin, trying not to seem like that was what he was doing. Sasha climbed up on the bed and curled into a ball at the foot.

The wind kept blowing, but it didn't compete with the blood racing through him. "Are you okay?"

William hummed and closed his eyes once more. He was not going to tell Garvin that he was awake because his entire body was on fire for him. Garvin was his friend, but if he didn't want anything more than that, then William wasn't going to make a fool of himself. Finally, at some point, he fell asleep, only to wake when Garvin got out of bed. The fire had burned down, and he added more wood, building it back up.

"It's cold again," William said.

"I know. It won't be for long." He got the heat building and then joined William under the covers. "The wind is dying down, and it looks like much of the snow has ended." He snuggled down under the covers.

William rolled over, pulling Garvin close to him, their heat combining.

"Hopefully the power will be restored tomorrow, but we'll have to see."

Part of William hoped the power stayed out. He could stay curled next to Garvin for as long as possible. But he made up his mind. No matter what, the first move had to be up to Garvin. If William made it, as he was tempted to do right now, he knew nothing would come of it. If William truly wanted a chance with Garvin, the decision had to be his. As hard as it was for William to be patient, that was what he had to do.

His mind made up, he closed his eyes and tried to fall back to sleep as a low rumble sounded—one he felt more than heard. Actually, William wasn't sure if he felt it or heard it, but *something* had happened. "Do you think that was an earthquake?" William had felt plenty of those in California, though this felt different. Maybe it had been some kind of winter thunderstorm, though Garvin said that the storm was lessening.

"Not sure. We'll find out in the morning." Garvin settled under the covers, and William let himself try to relax into sleep, but a second rumble, this one more intense, shook him, rattling a few of the dishes in the kitchen. It lasted for a few minutes, not growing, but the sound ebbing and flowing before dying away. Garvin didn't even wake, and once the sound had faded, he heard no more and finally fell to sleep.

THE ROAR of engines outside pulled him out of sleep. It was dark yet. Garvin still slept as William got up and added wood to the stove. The cabin was warmer, and the clock on the stove blinked. At some point in the night, the power must have been restored. That was good. At least they had basic heat and lights again. William went to the kitchen window to check out the noise and saw four men climbing off snowmobiles outside.

"Garvin, something is going on," he called.

"What?" he mumbled. "What do you need?"

"There's a group of guys outside." Even though he knew they were there, the loud knock on the door made him startle. Garvin got up, and William hurried over and opened the door before stepping back out of the cold.

"Enrique, what's going on?" Garvin asked.

"We need your help. There was a huge avalanche along one of the sides of the pass. Didn't you feel it?" Enrique asked.

"I think I did," William said. "I wondered if it was an earthquake."

"It was. That started the avalanche, and it buried some people. There are still three missing. We'll wait outside for you." Enrique closed the door behind him as Garvin raced into the bedroom.

"Stay here and keep the fire going. I don't know how long I'll be gone."

William followed him into the bedroom. "I'm going too." He had no intention of staying here alone all day, and if he could be of some help, then he would be. He pulled on the long underwear he'd bought and then a pair of jeans.

"I don't think that's a good idea. What do you know about winter rescue? About winter at all?" Now Garvin was being snide, and William glared at him.

"I know enough to keep my eyes open and watch for signs of people. You need to drive that snow beast, so I can be the lookout. Unless you want me to do the driving." He instantly saw Garvin tense. "Okay, then. Don't argue. You're wasting time." William pulled on a long-sleeve shirt and then a sweatshirt before stepping into his snow pants. He was already getting warm, but he got his coat on and then two pair of heavy socks before stepping into his boots and lacing them up tight. Finally, he pulled on the heavy hat he'd gotten and then lifted the hood from his coat in place. He probably looked like the kid from *A Christmas Story*.

"Fine. Wear these too. They will help you see and protect your eyes." Garvin handed him a pair of goggles. Then he pulled the strings on William's hood, bringing it closed, leaving just enough space for him to see and breathe. After doing the same for himself, Garvin told Sasha to be good, and then they tromped outside as William wondered what his impulsiveness and stubbornness had gotten him into this time.

CHAPTER 7

GARVIN HANDED William the helmet and had him put it on over his thick hat. Then he hurried back inside and returned with blankets, water, and rescue gear, which he placed in the insulated box. As soon as he raised his hand as a go signal, everyone took off. It had been less than ten minutes since that knock on the door, and he was damned impressed that William not only understood the urgency of the situation but got ready so fast.

"Where are we going?" William asked, holding him tightly around the waist.

Without slowing down, Garvin pointed toward the peaks just west and north of the trading post. When they reached the trading post, Enrique topped off all the tanks, and then they were off, screaming down little-used paths that got them to the base of the pass faster than if they had used the roads. Others joined them, probably from the forest service search and rescue.

"The missing people are the caretakers at a mining camp eight miles up the pass. The remains of the buildings have been found, but they were strewn over a large area." Enrique spread a map over the seat of his snowmobile. "We need teams of two, and the areas have been divided. We'll head up until this point."

Garvin knew the area well and nodded, his mind already plotting the directions.

"After that, we'll fan out. Go no farther than two miles, otherwise you could get too low on fuel. Return here after you've searched."

Enrique passed out radios, and William took theirs. "Check in every fifteen minutes and report your position. This is dangerous, and we don't want to add to the rescue. Does everyone understand?" He passed out maps as well. William tucked one in an outer pocket of his coat, shaking a little.

Garvin noticed the shiver and said, "If you're cold, you can stay here."

William got on the snowmobile. "Not cold. Just excited and ready to go." He patted the seat, and Garvin shook his head. This was the last reaction he had expected. William was really surprising him.

"Fine. But stay with me, and under no circumstances are you to go off on your own." Maybe he was stupid for bringing William along, but he took solace in the fact that the most likely areas would be taken by the forest service and the local volunteers would be searching the outlying areas just in case. It wasn't likely they would actually find anything, and this was largely going to be a long snowmobile ride.

"Got it. Do you know the way?" William asked, and Garvin nodded. "Then let's go." William pulled everything down tight, and Garvin started the snowmobile forward.

The sky was clear and the air cold and dry. He was grateful his goggles were tinted; otherwise he'd be completely blind in the glare off the snow. To save time, Garvin pushed the snowmobile as fast as he dared, reaching the meeting point in about twenty minutes. "Tell everyone that Ghost and Mr. Chicken have reached the meeting point and are heading out."

"Who?" William asked.

"That's us."

William pulled out the radio and sent the message. "And I'm the ghost. You can be Mr. Chicken." He put the radio away once they had been acknowledged. "There's someone else coming." He pointed, and Garvin looked, but it took a few seconds before he heard the engine. Damn, William must have bat hearing or something. "That's Enrique. He's going to be our other half."

William waved, and they got one in return. Enrique signaled, and Garvin took off to their assigned area. "I'm glad the engine is under us. It's keeping my butt warm."

Garvin smiled as they continued farther into the wilderness.

There was a road, but it was closed and under feet of snow, so for now, this area had reverted almost completely to nature. Enrique pointed and veered off. Garvin followed, going as fast as he dared. William held on tight, not saying anything. After a few minutes, they reached what had to be the leading edge of the avalanche.

"Jesus," William said, pointing to where the snow had come down, cutting a huge swath through the landscape. "Can anyone survive that?"

"We have to try to find out." Garvin continued forward and heard William call in that they had reached their area. He nodded and smiled to himself. William seemed to have picked up on what they needed to do.

"Do you see anything?" Enrique asked. Garvin shook his head.

"Turn off the engines," William said loudly. Garvin switched off his machine, and Enrique did the same. Instantly, the area turned quiet, with only the breeze and the snap of branches that gave up under the weight of the snow. William went stock-still, turning his head. "Okay, let's go."

"What are you doing?" Enrique asked.

William leaned closer. "In all this mess, it isn't likely we're going to see anything unless it's a bright coat color. There's too much jumble in the landscape. But we might hear something."

Enrique nodded and then pointed, and they were off again.

They made a large circle of their search area, stopping every few minutes to listen before continuing on. "There," William said, pointing as they neared the end of their loop.

"I don't hear anything," Enrique said.

"Over there," William insisted. Garvin started the engine and slowly headed in that direction. "Stop."

Garvin turned off the engine, and William pointed once again. "I'm hearing something on the wind from over there." He pointed once more and then stilled. This time Garvin heard it as well. He wasn't sure if it was a voice, but Enrique nodded, started the engine, and continued forward.

"There." Enrique pointed, and sure enough, something yellow marred the snow. "Stay here." Enrique grabbed snowshoes from the back of his snowmobile, and William radioed in that they might have found something.

Garvin carefully moved forward, and Enrique waved his arms before hurrying back. "It's all three of them, and they are definitely injured."

William immediately called it in and then handed the radio over. Garvin detailed the GPS coordinates. "We're going to need a chopper.

We have all three, but they are injured and probably suffering from exposure." Garvin had no idea how they got all this way, but avalanches had been known to carry people and debris for miles.

"We're converging on your coordinates. We have a helicopter on the way."

"Excellent, we are rendering what aid we can." Garvin handed William the radio and carefully made his way around him to the insulated box. He handed William a bottle of water. "Drink all of it." Garvin saved one for himself and then wrapped the others in the blankets and handed the bundle to Enrique, who moved his snowmobile closer to the men. Garvin followed.

"Okay. Stay here and man the radio. I'm going to help Enrique." He stepped off the snowmobile and sank nearly to his waist. He had expected it, and he propelled himself forward toward a depression the caretaking crew had managed to dig out for themselves to be able to sit, pushing the packed and jumbled snow behind him in a swimming motion.

Garvin handed out blankets for additional warmth and got them all wrapped up. "He's the worst," the smallest of the three men said, pointing to a taller man. "I think my leg is broken, Claude dislocated his arm, and Mark probably has cracked or broken ribs. We managed to stay together as the snow rolled us like laundry."

"Okay. We have help on the way." Garvin gave them all some water and helped them all share warmth until more snowmobiles sounded in the distance, followed by a second one with more blankets and supplies as well as an EMT, who took charge. Garvin stood, peering out of the depression, taking in the surrounding devastation. Trees, boulders, and chunks of wood from buildings stuck out at random intervals from the sometimes-dirt-strewn snow. It was a miracle they all survived.

Something caught Garvin's eye up the slope, and he tried to see it more clearly, but the light was fading as clouds rolled in. He gave up when a whoop-whoop sound indicated the rescue helicopter was approaching.

"We'll guide in the chopper," the other team said through the radio. "Need to move fast. Another front is expected."

Everyone worked quickly. EMTs from the chopper arrived on snowshoes, bringing baskets to get everyone out and transported by snowmobile to the chopper. Once the injured were on board, Garvin gathered everything and climbed out and onto the snowmobile, moving it away from the depression and pointing it toward home.

"You did amazing," he told William.

Enrique pulled up next to them. "Head back to the trading post. Angie will have hot sandwiches, soup, and plenty of coffee waiting." He took off, and Garvin made sure William was all set before they began the ride back, with Garvin closely watching the fuel. They had burned more than they should have, and the needle hovered at empty as they broke out of the trees just across the field from the trading post. He swore they glided the last bit of the way before he turned off the engine outside the main door, parking next to the group of others.

Garvin sighed and climbed off the snowmobile, his legs aching as he took the first steps toward the door. The sun from earlier was gone. Clouds had rolled in and hung low over the lake. As William joined him, the first flakes began to fall. At least with some cloud cover, it wouldn't get as cold. The worst were the clear nights, when it could get far below zero. "Let's get inside, get warm, and then we can put gas in the tank and go home."

"I take it you're tired," William said, apparently still filled with energy. Sometimes Garvin wondered where all of it came from.

"Let's go inside." He pulled off his helmet and took William's, and then they headed inside. As soon as they stepped through the small vestibule and into the main room of the post, applause broke out. Devon and the other guys began patting William on the back.

"That was good hunting," Enrique told him. "I never would have found them, but you heard something, and there they were." It turned out that the injured men had heard the snowmobiles and called out, but they couldn't be heard over the engines.

"I always had really good hearing." William took off his hat and outer layer and hung them on a hook. Garvin did the same, and then they sat at a table while Angie brought soup, coffee, and big subs that they practically inhaled.

"I just heard that all three of the folks we rescued are going to be okay. Their bones have been set, and they were treated for exposure, but they should all recover." Devon patted William's shoulder before moving on to make sure everyone had what they needed.

Garvin sat back in his chair, watching William soak up the attention, his cheeks flushing every time he received a compliment. "It was Enrique and Garvin who did the heavy work," he said. "They actually knew what to do to help them." He ate the rest of his soup, and for the first time, Garvin saw William in a different light.

He had always thought of William as attention-seeking. The guy made a career of walking runways and spending time in front of the camera doing commercials. He practically screamed "look at me." But maybe that was just an impression Garvin had. William could have hammed it up and made the most of his notoriety, but instead he seemed uncomfortable and kept throwing the light onto others.

"I'm really tired now that I've eaten." The day seemed to have passed in a flash. "We should get back to make sure Sasha is okay. I put some food in his dish before we left and made sure he had water, but I bet he needs to go out and should be fed again."

"Okay."

Garvin finished the last of his coffee and then thanked Enrique for the food and headed for the door to put on his gear. William did the same, receiving pats on the back and big smiles from everyone. Garvin huffed to himself as he yanked on his snow pants. He needed to stop himself from falling into old patterns, but it was hard. They had all worked together to help the avalanche victims. He pulled on his coat and hat, making sure everything was in place. Then, without waiting for William, he stomped out into the snow.

He checked the tank on the snowmobile, surprised and pleased to find it full. After climbing on, he started the engine and backed the machine away from the others. William came out and got on behind him. As soon as his arms slid around his waist, Garvin started the machine forward, heading south along the shoulder of the highway then turning down the lake road. He said nothing, stewing in his own juices, and the shitty thing was, he didn't know why.

So what if William had actually found the people? They needed help, and William's keen hearing had been instrumental in locating them. That was something Garvin should be happy about, not all roiled up inside over. He turned on the headlights and continued driving until he pulled the snow machine to a stop next to the cabin. Once they were off and the box emptied, William went inside, and Garvin covered the snowmobile and grabbed a load of wood to carry into the cabin.

William already had his outer gear off and was feeding Sasha, who sat next to William, looking up at him like he was the center of the world. Garvin got his gear off and then lit the fire, adding small pieces of wood to get it going and burning well. Then he added some logs and closed the stove door.

William took off the rest of his gear and hung it all up before grabbing two beers and flopping down on the sofa. Sasha curled up next to him, his head on William's lap. It seemed like William was everyone's man of the hour.

"What's up with you?" William asked. "You're never this quiet." He took a swig of beer and handed Garvin the second bottle. "We did good. You should be happy."

The shitty thing was that Garvin knew he should be pleased. They had found the folks who were missing, and in the end everything had turned out okay. That wasn't always the case in a situation like that. Often, search and rescue operations in severe cold weather found nothing… or weren't in time. But he was all twisted up. "I'm fine." He opened the beer and took a good swig.

"Bullshit," William countered. "You are not. I've known you long enough to know when you have your panties in a wad, and right now they're so tight, they're cutting off circulation to your balls." His glare grew colder than the air outside.

"I don't fucking get it, okay?"

"What's there to get? We did good—we found them."

Garvin scoffed. "You found them," he muttered.

William shrugged. "I heard them. Big deal. You and Enrique developed the pattern we followed to cover the entire search area. That brought us close enough that I could hear them. So big deal. Is that what has you all tied up? That the greenhorn who doesn't know anything up here actually located them?" He stared blankly at Garvin. "I never pictured you as an ass before. You can be a jerk sometimes and a definite PITA, but a real ass… nope."

"I am not," Garvin growled.

"Then get over yourself. We worked together and found them. That's good and what we were out there for. So what if everyone thinks I did something special? I actually contributed to the team instead of just warming the snowmobile seat with my ass." William set his bottle on the scarred coffee table. "Everyone was happy because the mission was a success." His gaze softened as he turned to Garvin. "Besides, the only person I wanted a pat on the back from… was you. Okay?"

Garvin swallowed hard as heat built inside him. William stayed still, his eyes filling with warmth. Was this going to happen? Garvin wasn't sure it should, but the pull toward William was becoming too great. The past couple of nights, it had taken all his willpower not to pull William to him, slip his hand under those sleep pants, take his cock in hand…. Garvin wanted that lean, luscious body, and he wanted it bad. He didn't know what to say. The current between them was too strong to ignore. He shifted closer, and Sasha lifted his head and looked at each of them before jumping down to lie in front of the fire.

"Smart dog," William said, and Garvin nodded without looking away. William licked his full lips but didn't move any nearer. Garvin found himself drawn closer, his entire body pulled to William by some invisible force that he couldn't control. "What do you want?" William whispered.

Garvin's mouth went dry, because he wanted William—badly. But he wasn't sure this was a good idea. They were friends, they had a history…. The one thing he did know was what he wanted. On a pure, basic level, under all this doubt and worry, he knew it was William that he needed, and as soon as he acknowledged that, William was right there. Garvin tilted his head, William stayed still… and finally Garvin crossed the last few inches between them.

Long before he had actually gotten the chance, he had imagined what kissing William would be like, but it was nothing compared to the reality. Garvin was transported. William's lips were firm yet soft, and he tasted and smelled clean, like the outdoors. William slipped his fingers

55

through Garvin's hair, deepening the kiss. He pressed Garvin back against the cushions, settling his weight on Garvin, and Garvin wrapped William in his arms and held him tightly as his head grew light.

"Damn," Garvin whispered when William pulled back slightly. "What the…?" He hadn't expected something that intense, and yet he could barely see straight… in the very best way possible. He hadn't experienced anything like that since he lost John, and it took him by surprise. He had never thought he would feel that again, and now that he had, he would have expected it to remind him of John, but it didn't. This was all William.

"It's really good that I can reduce you to incoherence. That's definitely a good thing." William kissed him again and then slowly sat back up. He helped Garvin upright once more and took his hand. He expected William to press on to something more, and part of him was disappointed that it didn't happen. Yet it was really nice that William seemed to want to take things slowly.

"What do you have as far as movies and stuff?" William asked.

Garvin opened the cabinet under the small television and let William choose something to watch. Then they settled in front of an action flick where Bruce Willis and his team set out to save the world. Not that Garvin paid that much attention. Sasha climbed onto the sofa again, settling on the other side of him, and Garvin leaned back against the cushions, closed his eyes, and let himself be truly happy for the first time in years.

CHAPTER 8

GARVIN HAD kissed him. It was a small step, and yet a big one, and from the way Garvin's eyes goggled, it seemed it had had as much of an effect on him as it had on William. And the interesting thing was that it had taken a lot less time than William had thought it would. Garvin was a thinker, and he mulled shit over in his head for a long time. But this was different, almost impulsive. Regardless, William was grateful for it, but he didn't want to push. Right now, Garvin was dozing, and after the morning and afternoon they'd had, it was no wonder.

He watched the movie and gazed at Garvin, with Sasha watching them. "Do you need to go out?" William asked, and Sasha perked up. William carefully got up, paused the movie, and let Sasha outside. It was a little after five-thirty and already pitch-dark. Sasha hurried out and came right back. William closed the door, added more wood to the fire, and settled on the sofa once again without waking Garvin.

Sometimes William wondered about his life and the choices he made... or didn't. It seemed that so many of the choices in his life had been made for him. Either that, or they hadn't been made at all. So much had fallen into his lap because of how he looked, because of how he walked... sometimes because he was in the right place. Things just happened. But this, with Garvin, wasn't like that. He needed to work for it, and he knew it was what he wanted. As the movie played, William sat watching Garvin and the way his hand lightly stroked his dog, even though he was asleep.

They had done well today, helping to save lives, but the best thing to happen was Garvin. He reached out, shifting on the cushions, and William took his hand, lightly caressing his rough fingers. Immediately Garvin settled back down and grew quiet, a soft smile on his lips.

Damn it all. William had tried to keep his feelings for his friend in check for years. First he had a husband, and then after John passed, he kept his distance. After that, Garvin had been so deep in his grief that he never came out. Maybe William was stupid to wait so long, but the heart wants what it wants. Now things seemed so close, and maybe he could have what he wanted.

Except Garvin was here in the wilds of Alaska, and William's life and work were in LA. Coming up here to find Garvin had been wildly impulsive and the best decision he'd made. But what about when his visit came to an end? Not that they had made promises to each other or even said anything that could lead William to believe that Garvin felt the same way, but there it was. William was falling right into his usual habit. He had completely fallen for someone he wanted but probably couldn't have, and there was nothing he could do about it.

Garvin started awake, looking around and then settling once more. "You okay?"

"Yeah, just weird dreams." He sighed and lay back again. "I was at the avalanche site, but things were so different."

"It was only a dream." William squeezed his hand.

"But it wasn't. I think it was my mind putting pieces together." He sat up. "On the next nice day, I want to go back out there. I want to return to where those people were found. There were things out there that weren't right. I can see if Enrique will go with me."

"I'll go, only this time I want to drive."

Garvin chuckled. "Maybe I can see if we can borrow an extra machine so you can have your own."

William shook his head, leaning closer. "No. See, I want you to ride behind me, your arms around my waist, your body pressed to mine. I want you to know what that feels like… for hours… and not be able to do anything about it." He winked, and Garvin groaned.

"I think I felt just how much you enjoyed that."

William cleared his throat. "Maybe, but mostly I was hanging on, afraid I was going to go flying when you went over some of those bumps." He hit Garvin with a glare. "Anyway, I'd be curious about what you might have found."

Garvin leaned forward excitedly. "That's just it. I'm not sure, but I think there were things there that shouldn't have been. But I was so focused on the task at hand that I'm not really sure what my mind picked up. While I slept, my mind showed me stuff that kind of makes sense… maybe."

"Then we'll go as soon as the weather allows for it." And just like that, he was volunteering to go out into the cold once more. He could hardly believe it. William had never liked the cold. He was a warm-weather person, but he was discovering he'd go just about anywhere with Garvin. "We should make something to eat. Enrique's late lunch was good, but I'm still hungry."

Garvin got up. "Me too. I have some things that I can heat up quick. Nothing fancy." He opened the refrigerator, and Sasha went over, probably to see what was in store for him. "I have some soup, but we had that earlier. There isn't a lot of variety sometimes." He pulled out sandwich fixings and set them on the counter. "In winter we tend to take what we can get."

"It's okay," William said as he joined him at the small counter. He made up a sandwich, but instead of beer, Garvin brought out bottles of juice and water.

"We need fluids, and beer isn't going to help us." They each drank some juice and then settled for water while they ate their sandwiches. William didn't feel the need to fill the silence with sound, and Garvin didn't seem to either. It was companionable and pleasant... until William's phone rang.

He picked it up, yawning. "Hey, Arnie." His booking agent. "What's up?"

"I have a couple of bookings for you, and I have three requests for Paris Fashion Week. Procter & Gamble is interested in you as a spokesman for a new dish detergent. When will you be back? They want to meet with you."

He sighed. "I don't know. Give me a little time. I'll be glad to Zoom with anyone and confirm for Paris, okay?" He knew he needed to go back eventually, but he had hoped he could have a little time away without too much pressure.

"I'll do my best. I can probably set up something with P&G for next week. But there are other potential jobs in the works, and they are going to want to meet with you before pulling the trigger."

"I understand." William met Garvin's worried gaze with a smile. "Just give me some time." He ended the call and set the phone aside.

"You still with Arnie?" Garvin asked. "I never liked that guy."

William rolled his eyes. "Really? I never would have figured that out. Before you left, you spent three years calling him Barney Blabbertwit." He had to smile at the memory, because Garvin had been right, Arnie did talk too much, but he got things done.

Garvin grinned. "I forgot about that. Thanks for reminding me. So what did the Barney of all Barneys want?"

"Really? Is that what you're going for? You couldn't have come up with something more original?" William loved the way he could tease Garvin and he never got mad.

"What? I haven't had any time to come up with better. I haven't thought about him in years. God, I would have thought that you'd have found someone else. I always like to picture him as the model for Barney Rubble. He even kind of looks like him: short, squat, and dumpy. All he needs is a club and he'd have the look down."

William stood close, his hands on his hips. "I'll have you know that Arnie has gotten me some great jobs. And I know he's different." He leaned right into Garvin's space. "But so are we, remember?" He held Garvin's gaze until he lowered his head slightly. "He's made me a ton of money in the past few years. Like, piles of it."

Garvin put up his hands. "Sorry. Heaven forbid I disparage the Barney." He curled his lips, and William lost it, collapsing onto Garvin as he slipped his arms around him. William lay with his head against Garvin's side, still chuckling. "So what did he want?"

"He's got some bookings for me. A potential commercial, and some gigs for fashion week in Paris. I'm doing really well. Photographers love working with me, and so do the designers. I have a body that they seem to design clothes for, and I'm easy to work with." He shrugged as Garvin pulled back.

His eyes widened. "I can't see that. You were always the biggest diva of anyone I've ever known."

William shook his head. "Let me ask you something. Would a diva come up here to the wilds of Alaska to find you? Or spend hours out in the frigid cold and snow to try to find people lost in an avalanche? I know you always thought I was flighty and self-absorbed, and maybe I was. Maybe I didn't think about anyone other than myself and damn the consequences. But I've changed. I grew up and figured out some shit."

"I see," Garvin said flatly.

William wanted to smack him, but he drew closer and kissed him, hard, possessively, like he had wanted to for days. He held Garvin's cheeks, taking control of everything as he pummeled Garvin's lips, giving him all the energy he had. Garvin seemed shocked for a split second, but then he hugged him tighter.

That was all the permission William needed. He tugged up Garvin's shirt and slipped his hand underneath, running it up his hot belly to his chest, tweaking those pert nipples until Garvin groaned against his lips. Then, just when Garvin writhed under him, William pulled back. "No, I don't think you do."

"What...? I thought...." Garvin whimpered, and damn, William liked him that way. His eyes were wide, and his chest heaved as he breathed. It was a damned good look on him.

"I know what you thought. But I *have* changed. I figured out some shit. I think things through now, in case you haven't noticed. I work hard at what I do, and success has come my way because of it. I don't spend my evenings out with the guys, and I don't go to clubs and dance the night away. I stopped all that shit."

"You did?" Garvin asked.

"Yeah. It was making me look old before my time, and I got this wake-up call. Suddenly the friend I thought would always be there was gone. He just fucking left." William growled as he squeezed Garvin's nipple, getting a hiss for his effort. "Damn, you like that?" He grinned. "Maybe you'll get a little more, but first...." He kissed him again, hard and firm, reveling in Garvin's fresh taste. "You need to understand. I waited for you. I had been for a long time, and then you never got over your grief. I wanted to help you. Fuck, I was always there, even when you called at two in the morning. But then you left, and...." William shrugged. "So I tried to be the person I thought you needed. I cleaned up my act and threw myself into work, trying to be a better version of myself. And I did it. I am that person... but you were still gone." He almost shook as he let all of that out. He had been holding it inside for so long that it poured out of him fast and with little control. Maybe he hadn't changed as much as he thought, though the old William would probably have blurted it out sooner.

"So you decided to try to find me?" Garvin asked.

"Yeah, I did. I figured you'd never come back, so I came looking for you… and nearly froze my ass off. But I came anyway."

Garvin swallowed. "So how long do you have? I know you have to go back. There are jobs you have to take, and your life isn't up here in the middle of nowhere, as you put it. So how long before you have to go?" The way Garvin said it made William think he might actually care.

"A couple of weeks. My agent is setting up some Zoom calls so I can talk to folks, but they are going to want to meet with me before making a final decision. So I have a little time." He hoped he got that long. Things had a habit of changing.

"I see. Is that all Barney wanted?" Garvin asked.

"You know guys like him. He'd feel much better if I were back in LA where he would know where I was and what I was up to." William rolled his eyes. "I think he figures I'm going to go back to doing things like I used to. But I don't think so. I'm not a kid anymore. I probably have two or three good years left and then I'll be too old. Then it will be younger guys who'll push me aside." If he was honest, that was part of what brought him here.

"I see." Garvin held him tightly. "You know, from where I stand, those young guys don't have anything on you."

"I wish that were true. But it's the way of things. Guys like me get older, and younger guys with tighter abs and big pouty lips or gazes that smolder on command are coming up, and they want their spot in the sun. Me, I've had more years in the business than most guys."

"Yet you still are in demand," Garvin pointed out. "So I don't think you have anything to worry about. But I understand. You have to make hay while you can."

"Yeah. But for now, I have a couple of weeks where I don't have to be anywhere. So if you can stand me for that long—"

Garvin cut him off with a kiss that stole away William's words.

"You can stay as long as you like," Garvin whispered.

William swallowed hard, looking deep into those purple-flecked blue eyes. "That wasn't how you felt a few days ago." Damn, why did he always feel the need to poke the bear? Why couldn't he just let things go?

"Do you really want to talk about this now?" Garvin asked.

William shook his head, glad that Garvin seemed willing to let this particular topic pass.

"Maybe we should head to the other room."

Sasha went over to the door, so Garvin slowly got up and let Sasha out for a few minutes while William added more wood to the stove. It continued putting out heat, and William stretched his hands over the top and rubbed them to soak up the warmth.

Garvin let Sasha back in and wiped his feet off. The dog made a beeline for the bedroom, and Garvin shook his head.

"Let me guess. He's staking out his claim on the bed."

"You better believe it." Garvin locked the door and began turning out the lights. "You know, going to bed used to be such a spontaneous thing when I was younger. No one gave a crap about lights or stoves or anything. It was all about the heat of the moment."

"Out here, I tend to think that spontaneous is probably not the best idea." Still, William took Garvin's hand and led him to the bedroom, where the first thing he did was kick Sasha out of the middle of the bed. "Is everything closed up for the night?" William sat on the side of the mattress.

Garvin nodded, meeting William's gaze with equal heat. "And the cabin is all set. There's nothing to worry about. It will probably snow all night, but the wind has died down again. We will be just fine. I can't guarantee there won't be some other crisis, but it shouldn't be of our making."

"Thank goodness," William breathed and tugged at the base of Garvin's shirt, pulling it up and over his head. "Because I've been waiting for this moment for a long time, and I don't care if there is a flood, an earthquake, or even a tornado...."

"I see." Garvin lowered his arms as William wound his around his waist. The room was chilly, raising goose bumps on William's otherwise smooth skin. "How about we get undressed and under the covers? Otherwise things are going to get shrively, and neither of us wants that." He pulled back the blankets before slipping off his shoes and socks and climbing into bed. William did the same, gliding naked under the crisp bedding.

"Dang, it's cold in here." He shivered and rolled onto his side. Garvin slid up to his back, pressing to him, spreading warmth that almost immediately stopped the shivers and added extra heat.

"Just give yourself a chance to warm up. It won't take long," Garvin whispered softly in his ear. Sasha decided it was his turn to join and jumped onto the bed, spreading out over William's feet.

"Your dog is a real cockblocker. I hope he knows that." He lifted his head to glare at the big ball of fur. Sasha blinked at him innocently before lowering his head to the covers.

"Sasha, get down," Garvin told him, but he just lay there. Eventually Garvin got up and led Sasha out of the room. William watched that tight butt bounce as he walked, then welcomed Garvin when he returned and slipped under the covers and into William's arms. "He should stay on the sofa. I made him a nice bed out there."

"If you say so." William drew Garvin into a kiss. He had waited so long for this, and when Garvin pressed him back on the mattress, his weight settling on top of him, William blinked and returned his kisses, reveling in Garvin's solidity.

"I'm glad you came," Garvin whispered. "It's...." He swallowed and seemed at a loss for words.

"I know it's been hard for you to move on." William stroked back Garvin's flopping hair.

He nodded, those big eyes filling with hurt for just a moment. "I honestly never thought I'd feel like this again. I thought that after losing John, real joy and passion would be gone. I doubted it would be possible to find this again."

William paused. "You do know that I'm not John?" The thought of being compared to a man who had been dead for years scared the hell out of him. There was no way he could compete with a distant, much-beloved memory that would only have become more perfect with time.

"Of course you aren't. John is gone," Garvin said.

William held Garvin's hand, his mood cooling. "I know he is. But is he gone for you?" He swallowed and blinked a few times.

"He's been gone for seven years. Yes, I've held on to his memory hard because I thought he and I were meant for each other. That John was my soulmate."

William sighed. "Maybe he was." Suddenly the bed was cold. He had waited years because he thought Garvin was special. Hell, he'd carried a stupid torch for him for years, and maybe it was all an illusion.

Maybe he really was the stupidest person on earth and should have just moved on. "And maybe your soul is already filled up." William got out of bed. He grabbed a blanket off the top and wrapped it around him.

"Where are you going?" Garvin asked as William left the bedroom.

He sat on the end of the sofa, pulling the blanket closed and his feet up so he was encased in warmth. What the hell was wrong with him? William was really good at going with the flow, but he needed to take a minute to figure out how things had gone from potentially hot and heavy to him sitting on the sofa alone in a matter of minutes. Maybe he had suddenly had a moment of clarity or finally held a mirror up to himself and realized how pathetic he'd been.

"William," Garvin said softly as he came into the room, also wrapped in a blanket. He sat down next to him, shooing Sasha off. "You know, sometimes when I think I have you figured out, you surprise me completely, and I have no idea what you're going to do or think next."

"Look—"

"No," Garvin said. "You need to know something. John was a huge part of my life, and losing him left me completely lost for a long time, probably longer than it should have. I'll admit now that I should have gotten help coping with the loss. But I couldn't. Getting help would have meant saying goodbye to him and letting go of part of him. So I held on to the grief and hurt because it was all I had left of him."

"I get that. But are you still holding on to it and looking to replace him?" William had always known that coming here was a risk and that it could blow up in his face.

"I know that I still love John and I probably always will, but it isn't like it was when he was alive. Like you said, he's gone and I can't get him back. I never could." Garvin held out his hand. "The truth is that I never compared you to John. The two of you are very different. You remember John—he was quiet, and he had that crooked smile he used whenever he felt uncomfortable."

William nodded. "He was also a complete nerd. He loved games and action figures."

"Yeah, he did. Used to drive me crazy." Garvin got up and went to a box on one of the bookshelves. He pulled out a key and dropped it in William's hand when he returned. "I didn't have the heart to get rid of them when I left, so I put them in climate-controlled storage before I left. All of them." He smiled and then began to laugh. "God, I am such an idiot. I thought that letting them go was letting go of John." He laughed harder. "I hated those damned things."

William began to laugh as well. "I always thought it funny that you made John keep them in that one room in the house."

"I told him he could have whatever he wanted as long as he kept it in there. I never did understand that part of his life. But I didn't have to. Those figures gave him joy, and he loved collecting them and spending his time hunting the damned things down. In the process, he made a fortune selling the gems that he didn't need. They were his passion—"

William shook his head. "*You* were his passion. We all knew that. John loved you more than anything else, and keeping those figures just demonstrates how much you loved him."

"I did… and I do… but not the same way I did when he was alive. John was a nerd of the highest order… and he was also the most passionate person I have ever met. No one will compare to him, but no one has to. John was an individual, and there's no one else like him, just like there's no one like you." He squeezed William's hand. "I love John, but he would never have gone out with me to look for avalanche victims. He would have stayed back here where it was warm. John hated the cold with a passion. When we went to Las Vegas, it was a hundred degrees. John walked most of the strip and was perfectly happy."

"Yeah. I get that. But…."

Garvin squeezed his fingers. "You will never replace John because you don't need to. These last few nights, I haven't been in bed thinking about John. I've been thinking about you, and when we kissed earlier, I can tell you that I did not even have a ghost of an inkling about John. It was all about you, your scent, the way you felt in my arms… everything was about you." He held William's gaze, and William could barely blink. "So to answer your first question, no, I will not be comparing you to John or him to you. That part of my life is over, and it's long past time that I figure out what comes next."

"That's good. But do you know what you want, or is this some exploration?"

66

Garvin chuckled. "Life is exploration. When I first met John, I didn't know what I wanted. I was in college and wasn't looking to meet someone who would be that special. In fact, we weren't at first. Things got off to a slow start for us, and the first date was a disaster. He spilled water all over the table and ended up drowning the pizza. It was a soggy mess. I figured that after we got home, he and I would go our separate ways. But John was nothing if not persistent."

"And you agreed to a second date after that?" William asked. Garvin was handsome now, and he had been back then as well. He could have dated any number of guys.

"I almost didn't." Garvin pulled the blanket up over him and then got up to add wood to the stove. "I didn't think he and I had anything in common. I figured we'd end up staring at each other across the table. I agreed anyway, and he took me out for fried chicken. We had a great time and ended up talking about all kinds of things. After dinner, we spent hours sitting outside under the stars." He yawned, covering his mouth with his hand. "He and I went out after that, and things clicked between us."

"I never had anyone like that," William confessed. "I had a few boyfriends back then, but they were more about the physical than anything else." He shrugged.

Garvin stood. "Come on. I think I've taken you down memory lane for long enough. Now that the weather has cleared up and power and internet are back, I have a class to conduct at eight in the morning." He stood, and William did the same, following Garvin into the bedroom.

After kicking Sasha off the bed, they slipped under the covers, and Garvin snuggled close, holding him tightly. William wasn't sure what to expect next, but he did his best to close his eyes and try to get some sleep.

CHAPTER 9

GARVIN WOKE to William returning to bed. "It's still early. I built up the fire to warm the place up, and I let Sasha out." He slipped under the covers, his skin cool to the touch. Garvin tugged him close and lightly kissed the back of his neck.

"Is everything okay?"

"Yes. It's still pitch-dark, and nothing seems to be moving outside. Sasha stayed out just a few minutes and is sleeping in front of the stove." He rolled over and pressed Garvin back, kissing him lightly. "Do you think that maybe we could make up for our interruption last night?" He kissed him, and Garvin hummed his most pleasant agreement, sliding his hands down William's back to cup his perfect behind.

"Are you sure?" William asked, and Garvin showed him by kissing William deeply. He was quite a man, and Garvin let his hands roam. More than once he had gotten a feel of William as they slept together, but he had always been careful because he didn't want William to think he was perving on him, even though he was. After all, William was stunning, with his highlighted hair, intense eyes, and fantastically lean body. Something about William really got him going, and Garvin wanted William to know that. He wanted him to feel it, not just hear the words.

"What are you thinking about?" William asked.

"How amazing you feel in my arms," he answered without missing a beat. "I was a fool to not have seen you for all these years."

William nuzzled his neck. "You see me now, and that's what matters. The past is just that, and neither of us can change it." He wriggled his hips, and Garvin groaned as William's cock slid alongside his own. "All any of us can do is move forward." He captured Garvin's lips and held him tightly as the two of them slowly rocked together. It was sweet and slow. Garvin should probably have been in a rush after all this time, but he didn't want to hurry William. They deserved to take their time, and

Garvin was a patient man. William was the one who usually rushed into things, and he seemed more than happy to go at Garvin's pace.

"Do you work out a lot?" Garvin asked as he ran his hands down William's chest.

"Yeah. It's part of the job description. Everyone wants their models to be slim. Hell, I swear it's the most unhealthy profession there is. When I'm home, I have to watch everything I eat." He smiled. "But I don't have to do that with you. I can just be myself."

Garvin didn't think he had heard anything more generous than that. Knowing that William didn't think he needed to put on an act or hide who he was was a high compliment. Everyone hid parts of themselves, and knowing that William had let his guard down was sexy as hell. "No, you don't. You open yourself in a way that's pretty amazing."

Their kisses intensified, as did the passion between them. The air in the room might have been chilled, but in that bed, under those covers, he and William scorched those sheets. Garvin didn't want this to end, but the heat built between them fast, and there was nothing he could do about it. The electricity between them was like a runaway engine, completely out of control with no way to slow it down before it overheated. William's skin against his provided just enough friction that there was no way Garvin could contain himself.

"Garvin," William whimpered, and Garvin gripped that perfect ass, clutching it as he pushed them harder, lifting William up as they slid together. He clamped his eyes closed, trying to hold on to some shred of control but losing it by the second. William was too sexy, and it had been so long since he'd allowed himself to feel anything for another man. Suddenly the dam burst and Garvin tumbled into sweet oblivion, taking William along with him.

He lay still, panting. "Damn…," Garvin breathed softly.

"I know. I guess there was a lot of pent-up anticipation on both sides." He laughed softly. "If I'd known that just having you in my arms like this would be so explosive…."

"I know. I wouldn't have waited so damned long either." He chuckled right along with William, closing his eyes and just letting himself be happy to exist in the moment. There was no need for anxiety or worry about what was to come next.

A bark, happy and energetic, broke their spell as Sasha raced into the room and up onto the bed. He pranced on top of the covers before jumping down once more. "I think someone is here."

"It isn't even light yet." William leaned over to glance at the clock.

"Yeah, I know. but I have to get up and start class anyway." He slipped out of bed, kissing William gently before heading to the bathroom, where he quickly cleaned up and then dressed before peering out the window, where Sasha had propped himself up against the sill.

"It's just snowshoers heading to the lake. They aren't here to play with you." He stroked Sasha's fur, rubbing him down. Garvin didn't dare let him out or he'd follow them, and Garvin didn't want him straying too far. Once he built up the fire, he logged in and waited as his students connected. Sasha put his front legs on the chair to get himself in the picture. The kids loved seeing Sasha, and they said hello to him as they connected, with Sasha barking his greeting back.

For the next few hours, Garvin conducted class, taking the kids through their lessons and answering questions. Then he gave them their homework assignments for that afternoon. Since they had been away for a few days, Garvin wanted to make sure they didn't fall behind.

"Let's go to the trading post for lunch. I have a few hours before I need to be back, and I want to talk over some things with the guys about what I saw," Garvin told William. "Sasha can go with us. It would be good for him to get out."

"Okay." William came right over and kissed him. "I wanted to do that all morning, but I didn't think your students would appreciate me making out with you during class." He smiled and then hurried over to start getting his outdoor gear on.

"WHAT HAS you so concerned?" Enrique asked once Garvin and William, along with Devon, were seated in the side room at the trading post. The walls were covered with some of Devon's local landscapes, making the trading post the closest thing to an art gallery in the Alaska bush. The thing was, folks had been driving up from Anchorage to look at his latest work and even buy pieces that fetched many thousands of dollars. Garvin had always admired the work and had his eye on one of the smaller pieces that hung on the main wall.

"Well," Garvin said, "when we found those three people after the avalanche, they were supposed to be caretakers at some mining operation. But what sort of mining is happening up where we found them? Think about it. You shut down an operation on the river a few years ago, and no new permits have been issued. I'm assuming that their camp was higher up, given the way the avalanches run downhill."

Enrique nodded. "There are still some old permits that are active, but they have mostly played out, and I've been told that they had largely ceased operations because they weren't finding anything viable, even with high gold prices."

William patted Garvin's leg. "What did you see that the rest of us missed?" He smiled. "What has you so worked up?"

"Well… you remember that the three people we found were in a hollowed-out depression and there were bits of the building they were in around them. It was all mixed in with the snow, and they used some of that wreckage as tools to dig with." He met the gazes of the other three. "But I noticed that some of those pieces of wood had been charred. They were black on the outside."

Devon and Enrique shared a look, while William gasped. "Which would mean that their building burned before the avalanche."

William sighed, his eyes as big as saucers. "Remember that night how I thought I felt an earthquake or heard winter thunder? In the morning I thought I heard the avalanche… and I did. But there were two rumbles, one sharper, and then another five minutes later that lasted longer. I thought the second was an earthquake. But what if neither of them was? What if the first was an explosion and the second was the avalanche?" He smiled, and Garvin tugged William into a hug.

"You're brilliant, you know that? And you're right. An explosion could cause an avalanche, which is why all explosives are banned in the winter. Mining ceases, and they have to wait till spring. Most responsible operations pull all their explosives because of the effect the cold can have on some of them."

All four of them gaped for a second at the implication. "So what if they weren't caretaking, but trying to mine this time of year?" Devon asked.

"Yeah, and their cache of explosives went off, bringing down half a mountain of snow on top of them. They're lucky to be alive," Enrique observed, but it was William who got to the heart of the matter.

"What if it's even more stupid? What if they didn't clear out their supplies of explosives because they wanted to get a head start in the spring, and their camp caught fire? An explosion would blow everything apart, and the snow and cold would douse everything fast, I'd think. So what if the fire came first, then the explosion, followed by the avalanche?"

Garvin nodded. "Either way, they are responsible for destroying miles of forest and thousands of trees, and God knows what else."

"True. But the only answers are out there," Devon said. "So what's the plan?"

Garvin leaned forward. "Tomorrow is Saturday, and I don't have class. My plan was to go back up there and see what I could find out. Bring back some of the charred wood as proof of what happened and see if we can find anything else. The longer we wait, the more everything will be buried under more snow, and by spring...."

"Everything will be covered by new growth, and everyone will have moved on to other issues," Enrique finished with a nod. "I'll make sure Angie can handle the Saturday breakfast crowd. We'll go on up at first light tomorrow. No storms are predicted, but who knows about the weather otherwise. At least we know right where we're going. We'll travel light and as fast as we can. Get in, take what proof we can, and get out before the mining company can get people in there, because once they do, everything that could tell us what happened will either be gone or lost until spring."

"I'm in," William said.

Garvin wasn't so sure that was a good idea, but judging by the set of his jaw, arguing with him would only cause a fight. Garvin would feel a lot better if William stayed here or back at the cabin.

"Are you sure?" Devon asked. "I know you helped out with the rescue, but tomorrow is going to be even colder. They're calling for clear skies, which means that temps are going to get well below zero, and even the sun isn't going to provide any heat."

William hesitated, and Garvin hoped he'd agree to stay back, but the set of his jaw returned. "I'm going."

Enrique and Devon nodded before getting up. Devon went back to his studio, and Enrique to work. Garvin and William ordered lunch and took a place at a table. "You know you don't have to do this."

William glared at him and leaned forward. "If you don't want me to go, just say so. I'm not going to intrude where you don't want me." Damn, Garvin was trying to figure out when William became so stubborn. He had always thought of him as this rather happy-go-lucky kind of guy that fortune just shone her light on. "I offered to go because I thought I could be of help, but if you think I'm just going to be in the way—"

"I didn't say that. I just thought that you might be more comfortable here at the trading post or back in the cabin where it will be warm. Sasha can stay with you, and…." He could see by William's darkening expression that he wasn't making any headway. "Look, this could be dangerous. We don't know what we're going to be getting ourselves in for. The mining company may already have gotten people up there to try to clean up their mess." The truth was that Garvin was concerned and just wanted William to be safe, but he was doing a shit job of explaining it.

"Sure. I'll sit back here and wonder the entire time if you've run into trouble or gotten hurt. You go on out in the severe cold and expect me to stay back here. If it's so dangerous, then none of you need to go, and you can all stay where it's safe and deal with this in the spring." Their burgers arrived, and William left his plate alone. "This is obviously important enough for you and your friends to go out in the cold to figure out what happened."

"It is. Mining is big business here, but it comes at a huge price, and the environment is what suffers. We put an end to an earlier operation, and if these people are breaking the law, we'll put an end to them too. Hopefully word is going to get out that this part of the state is just too expensive and that their kind isn't wanted. The rivers and streams in this area are clean, and we want to keep them that way. In the spring, the pass over the mountains is glorious with wildflowers and covered with tundra grass that wildlife feed on. We want all of it to remain that way."

William put up his hands. "I get it. You want to keep this area wild and as natural as possible."

"Exactly. We have osprey and hawks, bear and moose, as well as tons of fishing and natural streams, and they all need to be protected. Besides, who knows what these people were up to? It's likely they already caused a great deal of damage."

"Then we need to get up there and try to see what's truly going on, and the more sets of eyes, the better." He was being stubborn, and Garvin, while worried about him, didn't have the right to tell him not to go. "I'll be careful, and I'll dress warmly. I don't want to repeat the night I got here."

"Me either." There was no use fighting over it. William could be an asset to the team. He had sensational hearing, and he was observant. "We'll be up early so we can go as soon as it starts getting light. That way we can get there and back and not worry about the dark." Though Garvin had plenty else to worry about.

"ARE YOU set?" Garvin asked the following morning. He poured William some coffee and had him drink some extra water.

"Yeah." He drank the water and coffee before pulling on his gear. Garvin did the same, checking that William had everything on and that he was bundled up enough. He also had the snowmobile fully gassed up. He fed Sasha and let him out and back in before he and William headed over to the trading post, twilight just starting to build in the sky.

Devon and Enrique were ready and waiting, and after taking care of final plans and using the bathroom, they all headed out, zipping over the snow, following the same route they had the last time. In case they got separated, they agreed to use the same rendezvous point before heading out to where they had found the survivors.

"It's right over there," William said with a pat on the shoulder. Garvin shook his head, and William tapped him again, pointing.

"The GPS says it's still up ahead."

74

"But that tree right there. We turned just past it, and that's when I heard them." He pointed again, and Garvin turned. He was sure they were in the wrong spot until he saw the bits of wood and broken building. They came upon the field where the helicopter had landed and continued on. William's directions and the GPS converged as they approached the rescue site.

Garvin pulled to a stop, and Enrique did the same. "It's right over there. We have to be careful. The wind has probably blown snow into the shelter they dug, and we may not see it."

Enrique motioned. "Let's circle the area. We don't need to find where they took refuge. Let's head up the debris field and see what we can find. Follow me, go slowly, and watch for obstacles." He moved forward, and Garvin followed, treading carefully over what seemed like a huge field of snow and ice. But he knew the avalanche could bring down plenty of rocks and boulders as well, so who knew what was under the pristine white covering?

They made a wide arc before ending uphill, where larger pieces of the building were to be found. "You were right," Enrique called as he picked up a hunk of wood, brown on one side and black on the other. It was about three feet long, and Enrique attached it to the light sled he was pulling behind his machine.

"There's another," William said. "Can you get over there?"

Garvin maneuvered, and William stepped over the side of the machine and reached down to tug at the piece of wood. He grunted, and when the wood came loose, William overbalanced and fell off the snowmobile and into a snowbank up to his hips.

"Don't move," Enrique and Garvin said at the same time. "If you do, it will only dig you deeper." Enrique came around the other side and got as close to William as he could. Jesus, seeing him buried like that made Garvin's mouth go dry, and he had to force his mind to stay clear. All he wanted to do was go in after him, but that was a terrible idea. Stay calm and think straight—he knew that was what was needed, but his mind screamed at him to get William safe. "Hold on to the side of the snowmobile," Enrique said as Garvin's heart beat a mile a minute. "Good. Now lift yourself up and take Devon's hand."

"That's it," Garvin encouraged, his heart roaring in his ears as more of William emerged from the snow. He moved forward and around in a circle, approaching slowly on the other side. "Devon is going to lift you, and then you can climb back on." It took a few tries, but Garvin could breathe again, and the knot in his belly eased once William was safely on behind him again. The piece of wall lay about three feet away, and Devon and Enrique got it on the sled, covered it with a tarp, and bungee corded everything down.

"My guess is that the mine building was somewhere up that way. We could try to see what else we can find," Devon said.

"Turn off the engines," William said, holding Garvin tightly. Garvin cut the engine, and Enrique did the same. "Listen. It sounds like someone is coming. I think we should get the heck out of here. I think it's a chopper."

"I'm taking pictures of the area so we can document where we found the wood," Devon said as they started the engines once more, and Garvin took off across the open field toward the standing trees. The helicopter grew louder, the sled behind Enrique's snowmobile bouncing slightly.

"There it is," William said, and Garvin followed where he was pointing.

"Hang on. We aren't going to stop for a while." Garvin was afraid that snow might have gotten under William's winter clothing. It would melt closer to his skin, and the moisture would wick away heat. They continued forward as the helicopter made a loop over them. Garvin motioned to Enrique to keep going, and they slipped between the short, scraggy evergreen trees.

"What are you doing?" Garvin asked when William released his hold with one hand.

"The chopper is right over there. I'm waving to be friendly," William said. "If we run from them, they'll know something is up. But if we look friendly, they'll discount us and probably move on." Garvin felt him wave again, but Garvin continued forward. The trees would make it harder to see them, but all anyone had to do was follow their trail in the snow. Still, Enrique continued forward, intersecting their trail out and following along that same track. The chopper made a final circle and then continued on.

"Good thing they left. I think they thought we were hunters or something," William said, holding on once more. Garvin felt much better knowing William's hold was more secure, and he picked up speed again.

"I think they wanted to see what we had on the sled. It's a good thing Devon covered what we found, but they can follow our tracks to the avalanche area. We need to get back," Garvin said. An hour later, they broke out near one of the roads in the area and headed right back toward the trading post.

"Do you think there will be trouble?" William asked.

"I don't know." Garvin was more concerned about getting William inside where it was warm. He could feel him shivering a little and knew the cold had to be seeping in under his clothes. As clear as it was, there was nothing to hold in any heat, and it would get colder, even with the sunshine. When they reached the building, Garvin pulled up to the door and sent William inside, then parked next to Enrique's snow machine and helped unload the pieces of wood they'd gathered. "Where do you want to put them?"

Devon and Enrique shared one of those looks like they were talking silently to each other. "In the studio. We can let them warm up in there and then look them over." Devon went inside, and they each carried in a piece. Devon had cleared a space on the floor, and they laid them out. They were very clearly charred on one side, with ragged edges. Garvin was no expert by any means—hell, he taught school—but these pieces could have been part of an explosion and fire before the avalanche carried everything away.

"What do we do with this?" Enrique asked as he stood with his hands on his hips, looking down at the wood like it was going to offer up the answers as part of a grand speech.

"I say we call the state police," Garvin offered.

"I have Trooper Nelson's card in my office somewhere. I'll go find it and give him a call. See if he'll come on out."

Enrique left, and Garvin went through to the main room of the trading post. William had taken off his coat and snow pants and turned them inside out. His pants looked damp, and he sat at the bar, his hands wrapped around a mug of coffee.

"Are you getting warm again?"

"Yeah. I'm okay. I stayed pretty warm even though I was damp until I got in here. Then the chill started to take hold. But I'm getting better now, and I figured I should let everything dry out." He sipped his coffee, and Angie brought him a bowl of stew, which William began inhaling. "I guess it was pretty stupid of me to go in the first place. I wanted to help, but it's obvious I don't know shit about life up here."

"Hey, you rescued folks," Claude said from a stool two down. He was an old sourdough and had seen plenty of winters up here. "And you learn. The biggest thing is not to take chances unless you have to, and always have a backup plan." He smiled, or what came as close to it as Garvin had ever seen on that grizzled face.

"You got good gear, and falling in the snow happens to everyone." Garvin sat next to William.

"It sure as shit does. One time I was wintering out on my claim over closer to Palmer. I was out working traps when my snowshoes failed. Ended up with the frames up near my balls and me half buried in the white shit. I had to dig myself out and work my way back home. I was lucky and found some shelter and was able to build a fire and roast the rabbits I'd caught. Got me through the night, and I was able to make it home the next day." He patted William on the back. "You had friends who had your back."

"That I did," William said. "But what would have happened if…?"

"Don't go borrowing trouble," Claude warned. "You're here and safe, and the rest you learn from." He turned back to his bowl of stew, and Garvin motioned to Angie and requested a burger.

"You did good. You got us to where we needed to go, and you did it by landmarks and trees. That's something even Claude here would be impressed about."

"For a greenhorn?" Claude asked, nodding. "That's dang good. Young folks use GPS for everything, but I know the land."

"Well, I still feel stupid," William said and went back to his stew. Garvin clapped him on the shoulder, holding his gaze when William turned to him. Part of him had wanted to scold him for overbalancing. Seeing William tumble the way he did had scared him. He could have gone in headfirst, and God knows what could have been under that snow. Even once he knew William hadn't been hurt, his stomach had clenched and his heart raced until they got William back on the snowmobile. He hadn't wanted William to go in the first place, not because he thought he couldn't handle it but because he wanted him to stay safe, and he'd nearly buried himself in a snowbank. If it had been deeper and not packed down by the avalanche, he could have fallen to the point that the snow covered him. That idea sent a frigid chill up his back even in the warmth of the trading post. Still, William was fine, and they had gotten him out.

As it was, he was still concerned about what the helicopter had been about and if there was going to be trouble.

Garvin lightly patted William's knee to reassure him. "The biggest thing is that you didn't panic. You kept your head, and we were able to get you out." He felt like he needed to say something to help remove that hangdog expression from William's face.

William gave him a gentle smile, and Garvin squeezed his knee before pulling his hand away. There was no need to make too big a thing about the two of them in public. Still, he wanted to comfort William as best he could.

Enrique came out from the back room. "He's on his way."

"Who?" William asked.

"Trooper Nelson," Garvin answered softly. There was no need to start a bunch of rumors and talk running through the place. There was already enough about William's mishap and why they were up there in the first place. No need to add fuel to the rumor-mill fire.

Devon and Enrique went back about their business like nothing was going on. "Are you feeling drier?" Garvin asked William, who nodded as he ate the last of his stew.

"Yeah. I'm okay. It wasn't all that much snow, but it's nice to be where it's warm." He asked for another coffee and a glass of water, and he drank the entire glass before sipping the coffee more slowly.

Just as Garvin finished his lunch, Trooper Nelson came inside. Enrique met him, and the two men headed through to the back. "We may as well hear what he thinks." Garvin and William followed them back into Devon's studio and closed the door behind them.

"What's this?" Trooper Nelson asked, looking down. Enrique relayed the story of the rescue and their trip up today. The trooper knelt and examined the wood. "What made you suspicious? Avalanches happen, especially in heavy snow years like this one."

All of them shared a look. "Okay," William began. "First thing, I heard the avalanche. It happened after one in the morning. I woke to what I thought was thunder during the last storm. Then, five minutes later, there was a deeper rumble that went on for a while."

He nodded. "And you think the first one…?"

"Was an explosion at the mining site that caused the avalanche itself. As you can see, the remains are charred. That had to come from a fire. I suspect that the fire started because of the explosion, and then the avalanche wiped everything away. All we saw were pieces of buildings, but Garvin noticed charring when we were up there during the search and rescue."

Trooper Nelson nodded. "I need to go back to my car." He left the room, pulling on his coat and gear. He returned with a heavy plastic tool kit. "This isn't going to tell us what caused the charring, but it will show if there is any sort of explosive residue." He wiped the wood like they did in airports and put the swab in a small sensor in the case. It beeped and flashed red. "Okay, I think we have an answer."

"Damn," William said softly, meeting Garvin's gaze. "I wish I knew what it meant and what they were doing."

Garvin moved next to William and slid an arm around his waist. "Me too. Who would try to mine, much less use explosives, at this time of year?" The only answer that came to mind chilled him to the bone.

CHAPTER 10

WILLIAM WAS glad to be back in the cabin, and the first thing he did after stripping off his cold-weather gear was wash up and change his clothes. Then he settled on the sofa under a blanket. Sasha pressed next to him, glad they were home again. Garvin built up the fire in the stove, and then he too sat on the sofa.

"I don't get it. Who the heck did we rescue?" Garvin asked.

"Don will figure it out. They were all airlifted back, which means there will be records and things like that. He was as perplexed as we were. We did all we could, and now we have to let him look into things and unravel this puzzle. If nothing else, Don told me the mining company will be fined for improper storage of explosives and environmental damage. He said he agrees that there's something going on, but it's likely buried under tons of snow and won't come to light until spring."

"Which will probably only end with a slap on the wrist," Garvin said and then narrowed his gaze. "*Don?*"

William smiled. "Trooper Nelson. I talked to him while he was eating before hitting the road. He asked me where I was staying and seemed really friendly." He knew when a guy was interested, and Don had definitely had that look in his eyes. The guy was handsome and really built, that was for sure.

"How friendly?" Garvin asked, leaning closer, his voice rough.

William snickered. "Are you jealous?" he teased, which was the exact reaction he had been hoping for, and it was gratifying. Garvin stared daggers at him, and William smiled as he pulled the blanket up higher.

"That's why you said something," Garvin said with a huff. "Was this some sort of test?"

William drew closer. "No, but what if I said you passed anyway?" He closed the gap between them. William was all churned up inside. It had been frightening getting caught in the snow, but he had also spent a long time on the snowmobile pressed against Garvin, with that engine vibrating under him.

He wound his arms around Garvin's neck, pulling them together.

"And is this my reward?" Garvin slipped his hand under William's shirt, warmth spreading from the skin-to-skin contact.

"If you want it to be." He pulled Garvin back until they were both lying on the sofa, with William pressed between the cushions and Garvin. It was like being surrounded by heat. William kissed Garvin hard, releasing all the pent-up energy and anxiety from the morning.

"Jesus," Garvin growled as he tugged at William's shirt, soon getting it off. His sweatpants followed, and William was naked. It didn't take long for Garvin to shed his clothes, and then he practically dove back onto the sofa. William could barely stand it. He tried to take in all of Garvin at once, his hands, his lips, everything. William shook with excitement, and Garvin seemed almost as out of control. This was no slow lovemaking, but a frenzied joining that threatened to send William over the edge. "Roll over."

William complied, lying facedown on the sofa. Garvin's weight settled on his legs. "What...?" William whimpered before Garvin spread his cheeks. "Oh my God...." William clutched the edge of the nearest cushion as Garvin thrust his tongue inside him, driving William to distraction.

"Hasn't anyone ever done this?" Garvin asked.

William shook his head, gasping as Garvin blew his warm breath over his wet skin. "No," he whimpered and thrust back.

Garvin took him deeper, adding more heat. A slick finger slid into him, followed by another, which retracted and then slipped inside once more, driving William crazy. His mind kept trying to parse the sensations, but they melded together, one on top of the other.

"Then I'm glad I get to be the first." Garvin pressed his fingers into him, holding him before leaning over him. William turned to the side, and Garvin kissed him hard and deep, touching William's soul. Damn, all those years of longing burst upward and out as he felt the warm feelings being returned, *really* returned, for the first time. William hummed his pleasure and gave himself over to Garvin.

William shivered as the cool room air reached his skin, but Garvin seemed to fill him with warmth, and he didn't care. All he wanted was for Garvin to continue, and he did.

"This isn't going to be slow," Garvin warned, his voice cracking, eyes dark as the arctic night sky. Damn, that was sexy, and William braced himself while Garvin hurried away and then returned and pressed him into the cushions. William gasped and pushed back against Garvin's heat as Garvin slid through his opening and then inside him. William's head spun as Garvin sank deeper, filling him fast. Without hesitation, Garvin sank to the hilt and then pulled back, rocking his hips.

William held on to the cushions, moving in time with Garvin, their bodies instantly at the same rhythm. "Don't stop."

Garvin sucked on his ear. "I have no intention. Hang on, because I need you bad." He was like a man possessed. He wrapped his arms around William's chest, holding him as he drove into William, sending them both down a speedway of passion without limits.

"Damn," William groaned as Garvin pulled him back, holding him tightly, his hands caressing his chest as Garvin took complete possession of him. William loved every second of it. Passion overwhelmed him, and there was nothing he could do but go with it. He knew that Garvin would never hurt him. Hell, he trusted him, and that only added to the intensity.

"Need you so bad," Garvin groaned, sucking on his ear as he rocked his hips, sending William into near oblivion with each thrust. He needed, he wanted, and Garvin delivered everything and more without William saying a word.

"Then take me." He pushed back as Garvin's motions became more frantic, his hands sliding downward, stroking William's cock. In seconds, he was on the edge, and Garvin gripped him harder. It took mere moments for him to reach the peak, and without stopping, Garvin took them both over the edge, making William fly in a way he had never done before.

William couldn't move, and Garvin slowly lowered him to the cushions. He groaned as their bodies separated. Garvin slipped away and returned with a warm cloth that they used to clean up. Then Garvin joined William on the sofa and pulled a blanket up around both of them. "Where did that come from?" William whispered. "I always thought you'd be a quiet… I don't know, gentler lover."

Garvin chuckled. "I guess I did too. I mean, things have just gotten a little twisted these past few days, and then you were… and I was… and…." He gathered William in his arms. "I didn't hurt you, did I?"

William scoffed. "Goodness no. I'm tougher than I look, and besides… that was hot." He snuggled closer as a wet nose poked at his. "Sorry, Sasha, there isn't room for you up here."

"He doesn't want to be left out."

"That may be, but I'm not having him getting in on the action. I'm open for a lot of things, but I draw the line at that." He smiled as Garvin chuckled. Then he told Sasha to lie down, and William closed his eyes, fatigue and warm happiness washing over him.

"I have to ask, but were things like that with…?"

Garvin shrugged. "Do you really want to talk about things between John and me?"

William bit his lower lip. "I guess I keep wondering."

"John and I were happy, and we had a good relationship. But it wasn't one that was filled with fire and athletic passion. John was much more… quiet and gentle in bed. He was intense, caring, and passionate, but also rather quiet." He leaned forward so William could see his eyes. "I'm not comparing the two of you."

William didn't think Garvin was lying, but he couldn't help wondering. After all, Garvin had grieved for him for a very long time. "I guess I'm worried that I can't give you the things you need."

Garvin sighed. "That isn't something you need to worry about." William rolled over so he could look Garvin in the eyes. He needed to see him. "I don't know what's going to happen. But there is something I learned with John. He and I talked about things—everything. The two of us didn't have secrets."

"That's really cool of you." William closed his eyes once more and rested his head against Garvin's shoulder.

Garvin tensed. "What does that mean?"

William lifted his head. "I just suppose that when you love someone, you accept them for who they are, and it's good that you're able to do that. I suppose that we all have things we like and things that drive us crazy." He shrugged. "What did John do that you didn't like?"

Garvin thought for a few seconds. "I guess it was that he traveled for work. Not that he went to interesting places that often. If I had gone along, I might have been bored because he would be busy."

"Huh. I always thought you didn't go because you liked to be at home." He bit his lower lip.

"What made you think that?" Garvin's eyes drifted closed. "I like to travel and see things. But he was always busy."

William tensed and bit his lower lip once more. He wasn't privy to the ins and outs of Garvin's relationship with John, and that was their past. It certainly wasn't something he should get involved with. Garvin's memories of John were happy, and he didn't want to upset that. The last thing he wanted to do was to tarnish those memories. But William knew that many of the places that John went weren't exactly boring. Like he'd told Garvin, he always thought he just wanted to stay home, because William knew that John had traveled to Las Vegas, New Orleans, New York, and San Antonio a number of times and always went alone. If there was a reason for it, that was fine. But William had seen John in Las Vegas once, and John sure as hell hadn't been working. He had been having one hell of a good time. William hadn't seen him do anything that would categorize as cheating, but....

He closed his eyes and tried to put all that out of his head. There was no need to bring any of this up. After all, regardless of what John might have done, it was Garvin's memories he was worried about competing with, not the reality. Still, he was lying in Garvin's arms at the moment, and there was something to be said for that. Maybe William needed to worry less and be happy with what he had.

"Just rest awhile," Garvin whispered. "We've had a very busy day already, and the cold will take a lot out of you."

"I'd say you were the one who did that." William kissed him. The room was warming, and he was in Garvin's arms under a nice thick blanket, his skin pressed to Garvin's, which radiated more heat. He sighed softly, letting contentment wash over him, and let himself doze.

A BANG ON the door made him jump. William peered over the back of the sofa to see movement outside the door's small frosted windows. "This is supposed to be the frozen north, and everyone should be hibernating for the damned winter." He searched on the floor for the clothes Garvin had so neatly stripped off him. He slipped them on and stood, waking Garvin, who seemed to be able to sleep through the zombie apocalypse. He handed him his clothes, went with Sasha to the door, and cracked it open to see who was there.

"Can I help you?" With all the bulky clothes, he wasn't sure who it was.

"It's Devon."

"Oh." He let him inside and closed the door quickly so he didn't let all the warm air out.

Garvin sat up. "What's going on? Is there trouble?" He still seemed groggy, and his hair was going in every direction. It was cute, and William wanted to smooth it down. Hell, he wanted to run his fingers through it while Garvin sucked…. William needed to get that image out of his head because he didn't need to display the excitement that image brought to mind, at least not at the moment.

"Everything is fine. Except you signed up for my art class tomorrow, and I was wondering if you could help me get things set up beforehand. I forgot to ask you when we were at the trading post, but things were a little distracting. I was going to call, but the cell service is out."

"Sure. I can meet you at the library a little after noon." Garvin turned to William. "Do you want to come? Devon gives classes for kids and adults at the library every few weeks."

William grinned. "Sounds like fun. Though I swear my artistic development stopped at finger painting." He was good at expressing himself in other ways.

"Great. I'll see you then." Devon turned back toward the door. "I'm heading on up the road to check on Jackson and Grace. We haven't seen them for a while, and Enrique asked me to stop in to make sure they don't need anything." He waved and left, letting Sasha outside with him.

"It sounds like Willow, Alaska, is turning into a real center of culture," William teased.

Garvin wandered to the window that looked out on the frozen lake. The first stars were already making their appearance. "We need things to break up the long nights. Usually I spend a lot of time alone in the winter." He spoke quietly, maybe pensively. It was hard for William to figure out what he was feeling at that moment, and it set William on edge because he wasn't sure what surprise Garvin had in store for him.

"I suppose. I'm sorry if I crashed your solitude party."

Garvin didn't turn around. "You didn't. Well, actually you did, but I'm glad. It's been nice having you here for a visit." William got it now. Garvin thought of this as a visit, something that would start and end while William was here.

"I'm glad." What the hell else was he supposed to say? "I have to go back, but not for a few weeks. At least that's what I told my agent."

Garvin nodded, continuing to look outside. "That's great." At least Garvin didn't sound sarcastic, but trying to figure out what he was thinking could be a challenge. Garvin always seemed to keep himself locked away, especially after John's death. William had thought after the past few days, when things had progressed between them, maybe something in Garvin had changed. He had hoped that he had decided to move on, and that maybe he would want to move on with him. But maybe all that was wishful thinking on William's part and this was only an interlude until William went back to LA.

He sat on the sofa and turned on the television. There was very little on this far from the beaten path, so he found a DVD and put it in the player just for something to watch. He chose *Knockout* because it had action and Logan Steele was hot, but he kept the volume low. He heard scratching at the door and hurried over. He opened the door as Sasha shook the snow out of his fur and then trotted inside.

"Did you have a good time?" Garvin had explained that Sasha wouldn't go far. He went to his water dish and lapped it dry before checking his empty food bowl. William gave him a handful of food and more water before settling in front of the television once again. Sasha joined him, while Garvin continued staring out the window.

William left Garvin alone with his thoughts. He knew Garvin well enough to understand that there were times when he needed to think. Still, he got glasses of water and silently offered one to Garvin.

"I'm sorry," Garvin said softly, his voice sounding like he was a million miles away.

"What for?" William asked, pausing the movie.

Garvin shrugged, and William sat still, petting Sasha gently. Now that he knew the dog wasn't going to eat him, the two of them had become friends. He was still leery of dogs in general, but Sasha was a good dog, and it helped him get over his skittishness.

Eventually Garvin turned away from the window, and William went back to watching the movie. He hoped Garvin would join him, but he went into the kitchen and silently began making dinner. William wondered if he could help, but Garvin had this big "I need to be alone" vibe, so William stayed where he was, watching Garvin between movie scenes, wondering what was going on.

CHAPTER 11

GARVIN TRIED not to think too much about his growing feelings for William. There was no need to get too carried away. William was only staying for a few weeks, and it didn't matter how Garvin felt or how much his heart seemed to be invested. He needed to keep some sort of distance or he was going to fall to pieces once William returned to LA and his regular life, leaving Garvin alone once more.

He had been fine for the past two years living out in the bush. There were people around, but Garvin had been able to choose how he interacted with them, and when he felt like being hermity, he simply stayed in his cabin or worked on the property getting ready for winter. There was never a shortage of chores to do, so that kept him busy, as did his teaching. But with William here, things had changed. He found he liked having someone around, and he felt more social and wanted to get out and do things with others. But pretty soon he was going to be alone again. No matter how he felt about William or what he wanted, soon enough William would leave, and there was nothing he could do about it.

It had taken some time after John's death for him to learn that the world didn't give a crap about what he wanted. John had been taken from him, and there was nothing he could have done to change it. Garvin's world as he knew it had changed completely, and yet everything else went on. It was shitty, but the way of things. Just like William was going to leave because he had to return to his work and his life, and there wasn't shit that Garvin could do to change that. It seemed the best course of action was to simply pull away and keep some distance.

"You're thinking way too much," William said as he came into the kitchen. He filled his glass, drank more water, and then filled it again. William set the glass on the counter before slipping his arms around Garvin's waist. He didn't say anything more, and Garvin tensed at first, but William was warm, and no matter what he'd told himself, Garvin relaxed into the touch. Part of him rebuked himself for it, while the bigger piece figured he was being stupid and told him to enjoy what he had while William was here. He put down the knife he'd been using to cut potatoes and leaned back. "I could smell the smoke and hoped you weren't short-circuiting something."

"Very funny," Garvin said, grateful that William didn't press him. Sometimes he simply needed to be alone with his mind as he worked things out. "I have a few steaks that I thought we'd have, and I'm going to make mashed potatoes. An old-fashioned meat-and-potatoes dinner."

William squeezed him a little closer. "I haven't had one of those in a long time. You know me, I have to eat very carefully in order to stay working, but up here I can eat just about anything and still keep the weight off." He nipped at Garvin's ear. "My mom used to cook this way for us when we were kids."

"Mine too. The only thing was that my mother used the instant kind, and I hated those. It wasn't until I was an adult that I had real ones, and then there was no going back." He continued cutting the potatoes into pieces and adding them to the pot on the stove. "I have some veggies in the freezer. It's the best we can do out here."

William chuckled. "I noticed that there wasn't any lettuce or anything fresh on the menu at the trading post either."

"Well, yeah. If you go to Anchorage, you can get shipped-in veggies and fruit. But a tomato will cost you three bucks and a head of lettuce at least two. Everything fresh is shipped in, and by the time we get it up here, there isn't much left of it. I have a couple freezers in the pantry that I use to put things up from the garden. I also have lockers outside that I can store things in. But mostly it's canned and preserved everything this time of year." He opened the freezer and clunked a huge bag of mixed vegetables onto the counter. Then he took out what he wanted for the two of them and put the rest back.

"Costco?" William asked.

"Is there anything else? Whenever Enrique heads to Costco, he usually takes orders for the rest of us, especially this time of year." He finished getting everything ready and got the potatoes on the stove. Then he pulled the steaks out of the refrigerator to season. He was going to need to use the broiler in the oven because there was no other option, as cold as it was outside.

William went around and sat at one of the stools. "I don't cook much back home."

"Then how do you eat the way you need to?" Garvin asked. "I know you were never much of a cook, and I wasn't either. John did a lot of that sort of thing. He loved it. But out here, I've had to learn."

"I remember that. Usually back home I have someone come in every few weeks to cook for me, and I order salads and things to have delivered. I'm often so busy that there isn't time to do much more than heat something up."

"I suppose." In LA, their lives had been about rushing and pressure. But up here, it was less stressed and more concerned with what was really important. Nature provided all the pressure and tension that Garvin needed. His first winter up here had put a lot of things into perspective.

"I can already feel the difference here. It's about survival."

Garvin chuckled. "To a degree, I suppose. But it's not just that. We still have modern conveniences. They just take a different form sometimes. We're closer to nature here. We live with it rather than trying to bend it to our needs." In the city, the river ran through a concrete channel, while up here, rivers ran wild. "Come on. You can help me with dinner." He passed William the plate of steaks.

What hit him pretty hard was how good it felt to do things together. That was something he had forgotten. He and John used to do a lot together, just simple things. William came around, and Garvin talked him through what to do. Occasionally they bumped elbows or touched hips as they worked, and Garvin smiled. He'd missed that sort of togetherness. For a second he expected the old longings and wishes to come racing back, but they didn't. What took their place was bone-deep contentment, something so lost to him he barely recognized it.

"WHAT ARE you doing?" William mumbled the following morning as Garvin tried to slip out of bed. The air was cold, and he pulled his robe around his bare skin and stepped directly into his slippers. "It's Sunday."

Garvin snickered to himself. "And we need to go to church."

William sat up as if he'd had a shock, the covers pooling around his waist. "What are you, my mother?"

Damn, that was a sight, and Garvin was so tempted to push William back onto the bedding. But after their acrobatics the night before, he wondered if William might be a little sore. "I'm kidding. I'm going to stoke up the fire and get us something to eat. Then we're going to Devon's class at the library." He shared a kiss and then hurried to the other room, where he built up the fire, thankful there were still embers left from last night. They dressed and had breakfast before getting ready to go.

The sun was bright, reflecting off the ice and snow as they rode around the lake to the library on the other side. Garvin parked the snowmobile next to the others, and they went inside and hung up their outer gear.

Garvin paid for the class and led William through to the community room, where they helped set up the easels and supplies. Most of the winter resident families were represented in one way or another. The classes had started out as a way for Devon to teach the kids of the area during the summer, but over time they had morphed into a chance for everyone to learn from Devon's amazing talent. Not only was he an incredible and famous artist, he was also a great teacher who had a way of explaining what they were seeing in a way that made it easier to translate it to the canvas.

"Is everyone ready for something new?" Devon walked through the small grove of easels with canvases already placed. "We've been working on the view outside our window here for quite a while, and we've painted it in many seasons, but up until now, we haven't done winter, mainly because most of us think of it as a lack of color. Lots of white on white." He turned. "But there really isn't any white out there. Look at the ice. It's not white, but very light gray with touches of shadow, light and dark. There are blues and grays, even touches of red and brown from the leaves that have mixed in."

Garvin smiled over at William, who had leaned forward, his eyes shining with excitement.

"There are even blues from the sky tinting the snow, and of course the deep grays and blacks from the bare trees and conifers. Every color of the rainbow is out there, and yet at first glance we see only a blanket of snow. So what we're going to do is paint the lake, like we have before, but I want you to use white sparingly. Let the other colors you see come forward. Then, at the end, we can add touches of mixed white." Devon demonstrated the concept he was explaining with a simple painting of part of the far side of the lake. He brought it up close.

"I never saw it that way before," William said as he stood there while Garvin began. Devon finished his demonstration and then came to help William get started. Most people in the class had worked with Devon before, so they were familiar with the medium and began their work.

"It's one of the beautiful things about working with paint. We bring out what we see, so the interesting thing is that you and Garvin can look at the exact same point and each see something different. A photograph snaps an image, but with painting, you can convey not just a mood, but an emotion." Devon helped William find his bearings before wandering around to check on everyone and returning to the front.

"Are you enjoying yourself?" Garvin asked as he tried to make the bare trees not look weird.

"This is great." William seemed very tentative. Devon continued talking from the front, demonstrating techniques before walking through to offer encouragement and suggestions. None of them were going to be serious artists. Garvin was certain that his paintings would someday, long after he was dead, end up in a thrift store at a buck each or something. But that didn't matter. He was having a good time, especially watching William, who held his tongue between his teeth as he concentrated.

"Remember that this is a learning exercise. Don't worry about getting everything perfect. Just paint what you see and feel. The rest will come." Devon continued helping them all through the two-hour lesson. Garvin got much less done than he usually did because his attention kept being drawn to William.

"Mine is awful," William whispered before he began cleaning the brushes and putting away the paint. "It was fun, though."

"Art has a way of changing the way you look at the world," Devon said as he came over to help get things put away. "Once you start to see the colors that make up the world around you, it changes the way you see everything."

William scratched the back of his head. "I don't get it. I mean, the snow is the snow, and...."

Devon smiled. "Come here." He led William up to the windows, and Garvin followed. "Look at the sky. Now let your gaze lower to the surface of the lake. See how the blue gets picked up and reflected back?" William nodded. "Now look at the edges of the lake, near the trees. The snow is darker, even though it's not in shadow. Light plays off itself and mixes together. In a way, it connects the trees, the lake, and the sky all together. Once you see that, you know that everything is connected."

"Wow, I never understood...."

"It's the way we see things. Light is more dynamic and complex than we think it is. It mixes together so that snow isn't just white and the sky isn't just blue. Nothing is that static or flat. Everything gets mixed together and affected by everything else." He smiled.

"Thank you. Today was fun," William said. "I don't think I'm ever going to make an artist, but it was amazing to try something new."

"Then the day was a success," Devon said.

Garvin left the two of them to talk while he finished cleaning up their supplies and set their work to dry. Once he was done, they got their gear back on, and Garvin followed Devon over to the trading post. They had a big Sunday lunch. Enrique usually roasted something special, and this week it was turkey. The entire place smelled like his grandmother's kitchen from when he was a kid. Nearly all the tables were full. Garvin joined some friends, leaving a space for William as he wandered through the post, looking at the small works hanging on the walls.

Devon joined him, probably explaining each one.

"It looks like they seem to have hit it off," Enrique said.

"God, I hope so," Garvin said.

Enrique nodded. "You want him to stay, don't you? He's let something loose that you kept locked up for a long time, and now you can't put it back in the box."

Garvin shrugged. "I know that he can't stay. His life is back in California. What is he going to do up here?"

"You made a life up here," Enrique told him. "You didn't think you'd be able to when you first came. Remember, you had planned to just stay for the summer? And then you found something and made this place your home."

Garvin nodded even as he knew it hadn't been that simple. "I found peace and quiet here."

Enrique lowered his head but still managed to glare at him. "I think that's what you tell yourself. But you became part of the community here quickly. You helped the ladies with the garden tour. You went out and helped the kids with their summer activities. You didn't do the peace and quiet thing—you became part of the community." There was something about the way Enrique spoke that Garvin should maybe take offense at, but he didn't. "You come to the trading post most days for lunch and spend the time gabbing with the other guys."

"Everyone is familiar, and they're friends."

Enrique nodded. "Of course they are. It's part of life out here. But what I think is that you're ready to open yourself to more, to someone special again."

"I suppose I am." He bit his lower lip. "And what if it's William?" He was the last person Garvin would have expected to capture his heart. William, who seemed to go through life moving the way the wind blew, regardless of the consequences, and yet things always seemed to work out somehow. When he first showed up, Garvin had wondered what the hell William had been thinking, and now... dammit, Garvin was worried about what he was going to do when William left.

"If William is the one you want, then make sure he knows it. Show him the best of life out here. We all stay because there's something almost intoxicating about this place. Nature is right out the window. We don't need to go to a zoo or an aquarium to see it. There are mountains and lakes, streams and valleys that will take your breath away."

"That's true. But...."

"And you can get anything you want through Amazon." He winked. "Except a bride." Enrique snickered. "Did you hear that Gerald Spinner looked into a mail-order bride?"

"You're kidding," Garvin said. "What happened?"

"I think he came to his senses before he pursued it. But he told Devon and me about it, and we told a few close friends who have sisters. They had a party and invited all the single ladies, and Gerald met Marie. They've been going out for six months now. See? We all help each other."

"I see," Garvin said. "But I don't think there's anything any of you can do to help me with this."

Enrique shot him one of his looks again. "Don't be so sure. Remember, no matter how things work out, we'll all be there for you. If we have to, Devon and I can have a party and invite all the single gay men in this part of the state to see if one of them rings your bell."

Garvin laughed. He should have known Enrique would make him feel better. "Okay. That's one option." The other one was Garvin trying to figure out how to get William to stay. The more he thought about it, the more he figured that a damned party might be the more viable option.

CHAPTER 12

"I NEVER KNEW how quiet life could be," William said a couple days later, once Garvin had finished his online classes for the day. "I spent much of the day reading a book with Sasha, and it was nice." He peered outside at the sun glistening off the snow before placing a few additional logs in the stove.

"That's good, because we get plenty of quiet out here. The first few days you got here were incredibly active for this time of year."

William sat down in the chair across the desk from Garvin. "I sort of figured that it wasn't an everyday thing for you to go out and rescue folks from an avalanche." He leaned back, rubbing Sasha's head. In the week he'd been there, he'd gone from cautious around the dog to them being good friends.

"Those happen, but usually no one is there for it to affect. This whole mining issue is a real problem. Enrique and Devon put an end to one operation a few years ago that was illegally dumping chemicals into the river. They found out what they were doing, got proof, and shut them down. We all protect the area around here as best we can."

William leaned forward. "What I can't understand is how shady people can get a license in the first place."

Garvin turned off his computer and stood. "In this state, mining is a huge business. We don't pay state or sales tax here. The government is funded by oil and mining revenue, so without both, the government has no money. Therefore they tend to be pro mining, and as long as a company pays what they're supposed to...." He shrugged. "Like I said, we try to keep our part of the state as clean as we can."

William sat back, closing his eyes. "I keep wondering what they were doing. It had to be cold as hell up there."

"I have a theory," Garvin said. "The area up in the pass has been mined for years, and so has the river, because gold is contained in the rock. If it was spring, I could take you up the pass and you'd see the old mines with their piles of tailings."

"Okay?" William prompted. "That would be cool."

"So, put yourselves into their place. Three guys were supposed to be looking after the buildings and equipment during the winter. But let's say they went down into the mine to look around, and let's say they found something. What do you do?" He drew closer, his eyes filling with excitement.

William took his hand, tugging Garvin down into a kiss. "I'm with you so far."

Garvin snickered. "Does talking about mining get you excited?" William drew him even closer. "Because that's something I never would have guessed about you."

"*You* get me excited. You're passionate about this place, and I like that." After years of seeing Garvin down and mourning, this was wonderful. A passionate Garvin was sexy as hell, regardless of the reason.

"I see." Garvin kissed him again. "Do you want to hear the rest of what I think?" William's eyes goggled and he nodded. "So I think that they found something and decided to try to get it themselves. If they discovered a vein and could get it out, then no one was likely to find out. They were all alone."

"But their explosion to get at the ore brought all the snow on the mountain down on top of them," William whispered. This had to be some of the weirdest foreplay in history. Still, with Garvin so close, it didn't matter what they talked about. William was warm, his pulse raced, and he was hard enough to pound nails. "There's just one thing I don't understand."

"What's that?"

"Why would the mining company leave explosives up there all winter? These are supposed to be caretakers… that's all. The explosives would need to endure the extreme cold and the dampness when the snow melts. You told me they'd remove anything like that."

Garvin nodded. "I agree with you. And I can't think of anything, unless they squirreled it away. Or maybe they found some that was left behind by mistake."

William didn't take his gaze away from Garvin's intense eyes as he closed the distance between them and kissed Garvin hard, conveying that Garvin could talk all he wanted, but what William really wanted was action—and lots of it. "I'm sure explosives are regulated and have to be accounted for in detail. I also expect that they aren't cheap and that the company would want to know exactly what was used."

"And…?" Garvin prompted.

"Either the mine had them working all winter, which makes no sense, or…." William gasped. "Maybe it's something else entirely. What if they *did* find something? Remember that the building itself burned. So if they didn't know what they were doing… or did and made a mistake and accidentally set off a small explosion, maybe it damaged the building they were in and set it on fire. They got out… but started the avalanche." That made sense to him with the information they had. "What I really want to know is where we're going from here."

Garvin put a hand on each arm of the chair. Sasha left to soak in the warmth of the stove. Smart dog. "I say we go on back to the bedroom and—"

Sasha jumped up and hurried over to the door, growling. Garvin groaned and went over to him. Sasha began barking, and William joined them. "What's going on?" Two large men approached the door. "Do you know them?"

"Yes." Garvin moved back and let them inside.

"Enrique sent us over. He tried calling, but the phones are still spotty. There's trouble at the trading post. Some people from the mining company showed up, and they tried to give Enrique a hard time and threatened him."

"Okay. We'll get geared up. Are they still there?" Garvin asked, and the largest of the men nodded. "Then we'll be right over." They left, and William began getting dressed for the cold. "You don't have to go if you don't want to. Stay here with Sasha if you like."

"I'm going. I was there when we found the wood." He wasn't going to let Garvin and his friends stand alone in this. "Sasha can go with us, anyway. He probably needs to get out of the house for a while." William stepped into his snow pants and then pulled on his outdoor sweater before his coat and the rest of his gear. Garvin checked the stove and closed it up tight.

"Come on, Sasha," Garvin called, and they were off a few minutes later, zipping across the snowpack. The light was already fading by the time they reached the trading post.

"What the heck is going on?" William asked as soon as they stepped inside. Garvin held back Sasha, who snarled. It seemed he didn't like the attitude either.

"You had no right," a strange man said, pointing at Enrique. There were three other men behind him.

"To what?" William asked loudly, using his theater voice to cut through the din of raised voices. He stepped between the two groups of men, who looked about ready to square off. "And you need to calm down, or Sasha here is going to rip you apart."

"They stole from our mining site," he accused, pointing at Enrique and Devon.

"And what was taken?" William asked, playing dumb but not giving an inch. He knew he needed to get them talking rather than pushing back sleeves for a brawl. "What was the value?"

"It was…," he stammered.

"Some hunks of wood, which have already been turned over to the state police. We can call them if you want the wood back." William glanced toward Angie, who nodded. "But I suspect the police are already on their way. And I also think they are going to want to talk to all of you." That seemed to take some of the wind out of their sails.

"You had no right," the miner said, weaker this time.

"That's for the police to decide, not you."

Garvin stood next to him. "That entire pass is public land. We are part of the public, and it's open. Besides, you should be grateful to all of us for saving the lives of your fellow miners who got caught in the avalanche." Garvin stood tall, glaring at the group of men. "Now, all of you stand down."

"But what about the rest?" the miner asked.

"What rest?" William asked.

The miner, with his scruffy beard and intense eyes, seemed less sure of himself. "We were told that supplies and other goods were removed and that we should bring back everything that was taken from the site."

Garvin shook his head. "Sounds like you've been played." He shared a look with William, who nodded. So much for the men up there being out on their own. It sounded like whatever happened had been with the blessing of management. William wasn't sure which was worse. "And you still need to speak to the police, because they are going to be interested in what you know. That avalanche, which was most likely caused by your fellow miners, did a lot of damage to the forest."

"Sounds to me like you all could use some coffee while you wait," Angie said and started pouring cups to hand out.

"We aren't responsible for that." The miner took the mug and began looking around at the others like he was trying to garner support. "We just work for the company."

"And they sent you up here to try to strong-arm us into handing over evidence," William said, folding his arms over his chest.

"That's not why we're here," he said, but his voice sounded hollow, like the implications of what he had been told and what he'd tried to do just hit him.

"Really? Four guys all come in here, throw their weight around, and now you say you weren't trying to intimidate everyone," Enrique continued. "Don't feed me a line of bullshit and try to tell me it's candy. That isn't going to go over. We saw something suspicious when we helped rescue your fellow miners." He stepped forward. "They're your compatriots, so you should be grateful to us for what we did, not trying to make trouble. If you had been stuck up there, it would have been the people in this room who would have tried to save you." Damn, Enrique sure knew how to get at these guys. "I assume some or all of you will eventually try to work mines in this area...." He let the rest of his thought hang in the air.

All of the miners seemed to calm down after that. Devon offered them a table in the side room where they could wait for the police.

"Is everything going to be okay now?" William asked quietly. "They seem calmer."

Garvin slipped an arm around William's waist. "It's going to be fine. I suspect that none of these men really knows what happened firsthand. None of them were actually there. They were sent up here by their bosses to do a job." He kept his voice low. "However, we might be able to find out from them what's going on behind the scenes."

William sat down, and Sasha settled at his feet, leaning on his leg, watching the other men. It was clear that none of them were going to be able to get near Garvin or him without Sasha springing into action. William liked that Sasha seemed protective of him.

"It's okay," he said gently, stroking Sasha's head to try to calm him. "They are just angry and talking loudly. You don't get to eat them." William leaned closer. "They'd probably be tough and taste bad anyway." He smiled, and Sasha licked his face. "You're a good dog." Damn, a week ago he never would have thought he would be saying that.

"Would you like something from the kitchen?" Angie asked when she came to the table.

William shook his head. He wasn't hungry at the moment. "Maybe some coffee."

"Bring him a hamburger and fries," Garvin told her. "I'll have the same." He leaned closer. "Remember what I told you about eating out here. You need to keep your strength up."

William rolled his eyes but didn't argue. Maybe he'd be hungry once the food arrived.

As Angie served them their lunch, Trooper Nelson and another officer came through the door. Enrique met them, and they spoke for a few minutes. Then the troopers joined the miners in the side room. William ate the perfectly juicy hamburger, watching the expressions of the miners as they grew darker and more sullen by the second. They must have figured they'd come up here, demand what they wanted, and easily take it.

"We had nothing to do with that," one of the miners said loudly.

"Sounds like these guys have realized that there isn't going to be any work at the mine this year... possibly ever. This sort of recklessness is likely to get them shut down." Garvin ate quickly, finishing his food by the time William was halfway done.

"And that's a good thing? Aren't the mines a source of jobs and people who pass through? They'd bring more business to the trading post."

"Yes, they are. But if these people are careless enough to keep explosives or to try to blast in the winter, then who knows what they're doing the rest of the year. Putting their people in danger isn't helping anyone." Garvin sat back with his coffee. "Responsible mining is one thing, but cutting corners hurts the people who work there as well as the environment." His eyes blazed with passion, and William took his hand under the table.

"It seems to me that these guys are getting much more than they bargained for." They were now writing out statements and speaking individually to the troopers.

One by one they returned to the dining area as the troopers finished up. Then the officers spoke with Enrique and Devon before sitting down at their table. "What do you have to do with this?" Trooper Nelson asked.

"Nothing other than we helped retrieve the wood that we turned over to you. Enrique sent some guys over to get us when the miners showed up. Basically we're here for moral support and backup." Garvin finished his coffee and sat back.

"Have you been able to figure anything out?" William asked.

"The investigation is ongoing," Trooper Nelson answered as William's phone vibrated in his pocket. He excused himself and took Arnie's call.

"What's up?" William asked as cheerfully as he could. He was enjoying himself, and the last thing he wanted right now was his real life intruding. But it was inevitable.

"Everything is falling into place. Procter & Gamble wants to talk to you tomorrow, and they'd like to meet with you next week." He sounded like he'd won the lottery. "This is for a national spokesman spot with multiple commercials. You'll be as big as the Whirlpool guy."

William couldn't help smiling. "Will I have to wear a costume?"

"For the kind of money they're offering, they could want you naked and you'll do it. These people have a huge budget, and they're willing to pay for you. I also have you set up for Paris and am working on other bookings for that week. So when will you be back?" He finally stopped to breathe.

"I haven't booked anything yet," William answered. "Text me the schedule of when you need me where, and make the meeting with P&G late in the week."

Arnie scoffed. "Haven't you had enough freezing your nuts off up there? Come home where it's warm and sunny."

"I like it here. Last week I helped rescue people from an avalanche, and I'm riding on snowmobiles. It's quiet and so beautiful. I'm sending you pictures." The truth was, he was afraid that if he left, what was happening between him and Garvin would come to a screeching halt. He had wished to have Garvin in his life, and damn it all, he was head over heels for him. Garvin was strong, yet caring and gentle, and just thinking about the man in bed, when it was just the two of them.... Hell, Garvin paid attention to him, and even when they sat quietly in the cabin, just the two of them and the dog, it seemed special. William messaged Arnie some of the pictures he'd taken.

"It looks cold" was all Arnie replied.

"So? It's cold. The summers in LA are beastly hot, and you spend all your time in an air-conditioned building. So what's the difference?" He stood near the windows, looking out over the frozen land.

"Okay. Whatever you say. I'll send you the meeting details, and you send me your flight information. I'll pick you up at the airport when you get in."

"Thanks. I'll let you know." William ended the call and found Garvin talking with Enrique.

"There's nothing more that we can do right now. The troopers will continue to look into things, but we can't go back up there now. Too much visibility, and the mining company is certain to have people up there cleaning up and getting their things out, so anything we find will have been sanitized."

"Okay. So what's next? They can't just get away with this."

Enrique shrugged. "There will be a hearing on the mining company's license, and we'll have to make sure that we're there. It's the one way we are sure to make them pay. If they can't mine anymore, then all their resources will be spent for nothing. Also, there is a fine for breaking the rules."

William sighed. "It seems so anticlimactic. I want some big finish with the mine going up in flames and the people responsible getting gunned down in a hail of bullets."

Garvin chuckled. "You're such a drama queen."

"But am I wrong?" William turned to Enrique. "It seems like a letdown, even though I'm happy that there wasn't any violence. But still it feels like we should do something."

"We can't, not now. The weather is calling for more snow, and that means that we'll be shut in again. All we can do is hunker down once more and wait it out. Hopefully this will be the end of these storms and spring will start to come." Even as he said the words, the wind came up and blew snow off the roof in a sheet of white that obliterated the view of everything else. "Whatever is up there to find is going to be buried under even more snow, and if the wind picks up, any indication of what happened will be covered over."

"Okay," William said. "But we can do something. I can talk to Arnie and see if we can get someone to help us fight them legally. The police are doing what they can, but someone needs to speak for us. The mining company will send lawyers and lobbyists to do their talking in Juneau."

Garvin drew him closer. "Us? I like the sound of that."

"Yes. Every one of us who wants this area to remain as unspoiled as possible." William looked around. "All the people in here fish, right? What if the mine damages the river? What if the avalanche hurt animals and other game that are just trying to make it through the winter? They were killed, and it will take time for their numbers to be replaced. So less hunting." He could suddenly see the various cycles of life that could be interrupted by carelessness and greed, and it made him angry.

Enrique patted his shoulder. "Go ahead. We could use any help we can get."

"Okay. Let me see what I can come up with. Arnie knows plenty of lawyers, and they'll have to have contacts up here." He pulled out his phone and sent Arnie a message, telling him what he needed. Arnie sent back questions, and William briefly explained the issue. "Arnie says he'll put out some feelers to see what he can find out."

Garvin leaned closer. "Do you think he'll help?"

William smiled. "Yeah, he will. Not only does he want to keep me happy, but Arnie is a member of the Audubon Society, the Sierra Club, and a few other organizations. He's a big-time tree hugger, so this sort of thing makes him really angry."

"Okay, then. We'll wait until he gets back to us on that front," Enrique said. "And thank you. Mining is such big business that it can be hard for us to make our voices loud enough."

William had no doubts about Arnie and his ability to be heard. "He deals with the sharks in the fashion industry as well as Hollywood all the time. Arnie is more than a match for them." He actually thought it would be interesting to see the mining company go toe-to-toe with Arnie and his people. After an hour, those miners would be more than happy to crawl into their holes in the ground and never come out again.

"Good." Enrique stayed with them until the troopers finished with the miners. The group then sat at one of the tables and ordered food. Apparently they were feeling more conciliatory at the moment.

Sasha stayed close, situated right between them, watching the table of miners in case they did anything they shouldn't.

Garvin gently stroked his head. "You know, Sasha is going to miss you when you're gone."

William smiled. "I bet he's just waiting for me to go so he can take back my side the bed." He tried to play it off as humor, but it fell kind of flat.

"No. Really."

William nodded. "I'm going to miss him too." And the truth was that he was going to miss Garvin so much it frightened him. But there was no need to bring that up. William had to leave so he could get back to work. He had responsibilities and commitments to meet. "But I'll be back," he promised as he looked at Sasha. "I won't forget you, and I'll definitely come back to see you." While he was talking to the dog, the words were for Garvin.

"When were you planning to come?" Garvin asked, his voice rough but soft.

"I don't know. I was thinking that once I get this deal completed with P&G, I could come up here again for a while. I have to go to Paris in April for the spring shows." His calendar was filling up pretty quickly.

"And when will they need you to start filming?" Garvin asked. William knew that once these decisions were made, filming began quickly because time was money to these people. "You don't have to answer that. Your expression says it all." He drank the last of his coffee and set the mug on the table. "I don't know about you, but I'm ready to go back to the cabin. I have things to do in order to get ready in case we get snowed in again. Maybe we can take a run to Anchorage to lay in some supplies."

"Okay." William wished he could see a way out of this, but his work was back in LA. Maybe this entire trip had been a mistake. Just like his friends thought he always did, William had rushed headlong into something without considering the consequences. He had come up here because he wanted to see Garvin. Things between them had progressed better than William had ever hoped... but now he had to leave again. His lack of planning had probably left both of them worse off in the long run.

CHAPTER 13

WITH HIS Jeep loaded with supplies, William in the passenger seat, and Sasha on one side in back, Garvin drove carefully as darkness fell over the Parks Highway. They had just passed through Wasilla as it began to snow. "This is just what it did on the night I arrived."

Garvin turned on the radio to get a report as he continued their trek north and west. "It isn't supposed to be too bad. These are the flurries coming in before the main storm." He hoped. There was a break in the programming as a voice confirmed that the storm wouldn't hit until later and that it wasn't expected to be nearly as intense as the others. That was good news. The wind hadn't picked up yet, so he had decent visibility.

"When we get back, I need to book my return flight. Will you be able to give me a ride to the airport?" The rental company had picked his car up, and William hadn't requested a replacement.

"Of course. Just let me know when so I can make sure I don't need to teach at that time."

"Most leave at night, so you can teach and then take me in. It isn't necessary for you to wait around or anything." He turned in the seat. "I meant what I said. I will be back. I promise."

"You don't need to put yourself out on my account," Garvin grumbled. He might as well get used to being alone again. He had spent the past two years alone up here, and he would do it again.

William snorted. "You don't need to be a jerk. This isn't some made-for-TV movie where one person says they have to go and the other makes like it's no big deal… for some stupid reason."

Garvin didn't look away from the road ahead. "What do you want me to say?" He needed to keep himself under control and his emotions in check.

"I don't know. What you really feel instead of some stupid front to keep from feeling bad? Maybe be honest and say what's really on your mind."

"Fine," Garvin snapped and wished he hadn't. "I wish you weren't going. Okay? Not that it changes anything, but I wish you could stay." There, he'd actually said it.

"I wish I could stay too. I like it here with you and Sasha, and as shocking as it is to me, I like going out in the freezing cold on the snowmobile with you. I like being here, and I like your friends. They're a great bunch. You have a good life here, and I'd like to have something like that in my life. But I have to go back and make a living. What I can do isn't available here, and I have to go where the work is. You know that."

Garvin knew William was right, and that was part of what hurt so bad. "But it doesn't make it any easier."

"I don't suppose it does, but it's not like I'm going to come all the way to Alaska to try to get you to notice me and then when you do, disappear forever." William looked at him like Garvin was crazy. "We'll just have to figure things out. Have you ever thought about coming to LA during the winter? It would be warmer, and I have a place there. You could bring Sasha and stay with me."

Garvin's stomach clenched immediately. "I don't think I can do that. LA isn't somewhere I can ever live again. There are too many memories there. I left to try to get away from them, to build a new life, and I did." Just the thought of going back had him gripping the wheel tighter. He breathed deeply, trying to stave off an anxiety attack. He hadn't had one in a long time.

"Hey, it was only a suggestion." William gently patted Garvin's knee. "Just relax. If I had known how it would make you feel, I never would have brought it up. I like it here in Alaska, and even in the small cabin, you and I get along well. So don't worry about it."

Garvin nodded, but he didn't know how things could work out. He loved his home, and this place was that now. It wasn't like he was holding on to John as much anymore. He was ready to move on, but doing it in LA would be impossible. Besides, he wasn't the same person he'd been back then. Garvin loved the open, wild spaces of Alaska. He could drive back roads and not see another person all day... and yet on that same road, he could see moose, caribou, and bear, and pass beaver lodges and osprey nests. "I can't help it sometimes."

"Hey. You know I have to go back and that I'm going to be busy. But things will work out." William sounded so sure of himself.

"I don't see how. What are you going to do? Fly back and forth on a regular basis?" He really didn't see how this could work, but he was willing to give William the benefit of the doubt. He had to, because otherwise he would be alone again. And that really sucked.

"I don't know, but I have to try. That is, unless you don't want me to." The soft hurt in William's voice was almost too much.

"Of course I do." Garvin made the turn and slowed as the lights of the library and community center came into view. He turned and made his way slowly down the road around the lake. He pulled into his drive and parked under the carport just as the wind picked up. They unloaded the Jeep, not saying anything more, and Garvin wondered if his own practical nature had only added more tension and anxiety. That hadn't been his intention, but William was quiet.

Inside, after they got out of their gear, Garvin built up the fire while William spent time on his phone. He spoke quietly with Arnie. Garvin put away the things he'd gotten on their trip and then began making a simple dinner. They hadn't spoken in over an hour, and Garvin didn't know what to do to fix it.

He and William had spent quiet hours together in the same room and everything was fine. They were happy and comfortable with each other. But this was different. The silence hung heavily in the air, and he wasn't sure what to do about it. What he'd said was the truth—well, at least what he thought of as the truth. Garvin wasn't very good at trusting that things would work out. In a bright blue sky, he was the guy who picked out the single cloud on the horizon that might carry a tinge of darkness.

"Garvin," William said, and Garvin set down the knife and went over to where William sat rigidly on one side of the sofa with Sasha pressed right up against him, like he was afraid William was going to leave at any minute. Maybe that was what Garvin was worried about as well. "There are flights back every day at ten at night with seats available." He seemed so tentative, and Garvin hated that. William was not that kind of guy. He had his quirks, but he was the kind of person who jumped on the back of a snowmobile to rescue people rather than sitting on the damned sofa, looking like he wanted the cushions to swallow him.

"When do you have to be back?" Garvin asked.

"My meeting is a week from Thursday."

"Then go back on Tuesday to give yourself a day in case the weather is bad. That will give you a day of grace so you don't miss it."

William lifted his gaze. Those huge eyes that Garvin had seen in commercials—eyes that could sell damned near anything on the runway—sent his heart racing. "Is that what you really want?"

Garvin took William's phone. "Arnie, this is his friend, Garvin. William is having a good time here. He's helped save three people's lives, and he's brought life and light back to mine. So get him on the flight that will allow him to make his meeting but will give him the most time here with me. Okay?"

A throat cleared on the other side of the line. "This is Sarah, Arnie's assistant." She chuckled. "And I'll be sure to do that. I'll text William the details, and now, could you put him back on?"

Garvin silently handed William the phone back and, without another word, returned to the kitchen, where he chopped onions with enough force that little bits of them went flying onto the floor and he needed to clean them up before Sasha tried to eat them.

"Okay," William said after he ended the call. He got off the sofa and came over to where he was cutting the already cooked potatoes. "I guess that answers one of my questions." He leaned against the counter.

"Just one?"

"Oh yeah. I have a ton more. Were you this big a pain in the ass with John? Why in the hell can't you just say what you want and not go in for all the drama? Do you really want me to stay, or are you just being nice? And does this mean you really care about me, or am I just a convenient way to dispel your own loneliness?"

Garvin smacked down his knife with more force than he intended. "I was not lonely."

William shook his head. "*That's* the question you thought was important? You really are a pain in the ass sometimes." He reached across the counter, grabbed Garvin's shirt, pulled him forward, and crashed their lips together in a kiss that made Garvin forget the rest of the world existed. When William pulled back, Garvin blinked and shook his head slightly.

"What?" Garvin asked as William stayed where he was, staring at him.

"I'm still waiting for my answers." Damn, William was feisty today. He stood straight and folded his arms over his chest.

"Okay. I don't remember the questions. But I clearly want you to stay."

"And were you a giant pain in the ass with John as well?" William pressed.

Garvin shrugged. "I probably was. And yes, I want you to stay, and you should know I never do shit just to be nice. You're not the best about expressing your feelings either, Mr. Silent Treatment."

William sighed deeply. "I told you how I felt already. I've hoped you'd open your damned eyes and see what was right in front of you for years." He rolled his big eyes. "I have to go back so I can work. But I told you I'll come back here, and I meant it. I traveled all this way to see you in the first place because you'd come up here and I was afraid you had fallen off the face of the earth. And I did that because I've loved you for years. Okay? You're strong and caring. You help those you care about without thought, and hell, you take off across a snowpack that goes halfway to Russia in order to help someone you don't even know. So hell yes, I'll be back, and I'm hoping that you and your pain-in-the-ass-ness will come down to LA to see me for a few weeks so that we can be together while I film these commercials. My place is small, but you can bring Sasha with you, and we'll take him for walks at the shore. That is, if you really want a chance for the two of us to see if this can go anywhere." His jaw was set tight, and his eyes blazed. "If you want to give this a try, then you need to do part of it."

Garvin picked up the knife but just held the handle in his hand. "I told you, I don't know if I can go back to LA. I left that behind." He lifted his gaze from the scarred cutting board. "I know this is hard to understand, but I stayed there for five years after John died and just wallowed in his loss. It wasn't until I moved here and built a whole new life of my own that I finally began to pull myself out of it. I had to start over...." He set down the knife once more. "And it wasn't until you came that I was finally able to let go of the past... of my past... and I don't want to go back there. I can't."

"You aren't the same person you were back then. You're confident, and you know who you are without John."

"Yes, that's true. But can't you see? John's life was back there. It was him. I was this kid from Oklahoma who moved to the city and got fucking lucky. I met John, a kid from Nebraska, and he took my breath away. We fell in love and somehow managed to build a life around and through school and his years of medical training and John starting his practice. It was the two of us against the world in a big city that sometimes seemed like him and yet not.... But in the end, it was always John and me. We could do anything together. But when he died, there was no more him. It was just me." Garvin tried to keep his thoughts from spinning out of control. "I tried to go on, but you saw what happened. So I left and built a life here. This is my life, out here in the middle of a small community that accepts me for me. They helped heal me and bring me back to life."

"Okay," William said. "I can respect that."

Garvin closed his eyes, breathing more easily again.

"We all have places that we call home, and this is yours."

"Yes. I know it sounds like I'm escaping, and maybe I am. But this place, with the lake and the trading post, the guys... and Sasha... all of it is home." He walked around the counter. "The thing is that you feel like home too. Like you belong here with me, and that's why you going away is so hard. It feels to me like I'm losing something all over again. You were that someone I've been waiting for, and I didn't have a clue until you showed up in the middle of a damned snowstorm."

William held him in his warm arms. "I will be back. This isn't the last of it. Because you feel like home to me too." He kissed him again, this time more gently, but with so much intensity and desire that Garvin couldn't help throwing all he had right back to William. "But we have to make the most of the time we have now."

Garvin knew William was right. "I wish I had done that with John." He began chopping again. "I think that was part of what made it so hard when John was gone at conferences or working long hours." He had never spoken about any of this with anyone. "I loved John with everything I had, but I think I was too selfish. John was always so easygoing, and he just went with things. I had my kids and classes there, and I had to be in school. John had his practice, and we were both working. John wanted to travel and go and do so many things. But I taught summer school because I needed the money to pay off my loans and stuff. John offered many times, and I wish I had just let him." He paused to open the refrigerator and pull out some eggs. "Six months before he passed away, John said he could get time away from the office for a couple weeks. He said that we should go to Europe, see Rome, Florence, and Venice. He had even found where he could make all the arrangements, and he was so excited."

William leaned closer. "I didn't know that."

"Because I said I had to work. I was teaching a special summer session. I could have gotten out of it, but I didn't. It was good money, and I was focused on wiping out those loans. So he let it go and never mentioned it again. Then three months later he was gone, a timebomb in his brain. If I had just taken advantage of the opportunity, the two of us could have gone and done things. Instead we worked, and then he was gone, and it was my fault."

William took his hands. "How were you supposed to know? You were trying to build a future for the two of you, just like John. You worked to help build the life the two of you wanted."

"Yeah, I know. But John always wanted to travel. He didn't get to do it when he was a kid, and he really wanted to see things. He and I talked about going to Asia and Australia as well as Europe. He really wanted to see the world, and I was busy working and could never get time off. And when John could, I was still busy, so he missed out on his chance. I don't want that to happen again. I want to make the most of the opportunities that I'm given, but I can't help regretting things. I made a bunch of mistakes with John. What if I make the same ones with you?"

William shrugged. "Then don't."

"It's not that simple," Garvin countered.

"Maybe it is. Maybe all you need to do is tell yourself that you aren't going to make the same mistakes. Let yourself be happy."

"I was happy, and I thought John was happy. But now sometimes I wonder if I stifled him and made him give up the things he really wanted." As Garvin thought about it, there was so much. "John had wanted a motorcycle ever since he was a kid. He used to have toy ones. The other kids had cars; he had motorcycles. His collection is still in a box in storage along with the action figures that rode them. I remember that the first time he talked about getting one, I freaked, because I had an aunt who was injured riding one. I didn't want John to get hurt, and they scared the hell out of me. So he didn't buy one. John made a lot of sacrifices because of me, and now he's gone."

William shook his head. "You know all of this is bullshit." The words and William's tone surprised Garvin. That reaction was the last thing he expected. "Total bullshit."

"Really?" He could feel his temper rising.

"John loved you more than anything, and neither of you had any idea that he was going to get sick. The two of you should have had a long life together. It's what you deserved—what all of us deserve and should have. But you didn't." William leaned closer. "So build a bridge, get over it, and go on with your life. You'll always love John, but you can't stop living or let your past dictate the kind of future you're going to have. Learn from the shit you did wrong and don't make the same mistake again. It's just that simple."

Garvin was taken aback, and he didn't know what to do with that advice. "Build a bridge? Never heard that one before." He chuckled and went back to making dinner. William was probably right—Garvin did need to figure out how to let go of the last pieces of his past. And he needed to do that if he could hope to have any sort of future.

CHAPTER 14

WILLIAM HOPED he hadn't gone too far, but Garvin kept holding on to his past like it was a damned lifeline. He was even trying to milk his mistakes as some sort of excuse for not moving on. Their friends in LA had treated Garvin with kid gloves for years. Maybe that was the problem.

"Dinner will be ready in a few minutes," Garvin said, and William turned away from the counter and returned to where Sasha stood on the sofa, looking over the back like he was ready to spring into action if things felt wrong. William stroked his head and sat down, putting his feet up. There was little he could do if Garvin wasn't willing to meet him at least part of the way. Maybe it was simply too much to expect. If Garvin was determined to wallow in his past, there was nothing William could do about it. Or maybe he was just too stubborn to make any sort of compromise. It wasn't like William was asking him to leave Willow and move back to LA, but a visit during the times when William was shooting and couldn't get up here didn't seem unreasonable.

He shrugged. Maybe William was just too stubborn himself and couldn't see that Garvin wasn't that interested. If you loved someone, you wanted to help make them happy. And William did want Garvin to be happy. So maybe he just needed to accept that they had the time they had and let that be the end of it. Any relationship had to be what both people wanted, and if Garvin thought he was only going to be happy here, then who was William to tell him any different?

"I'm almost finished with the frittatas," Garvin said. William joined him, getting out the plates and things for dinner. There was no use fighting. He was only here for a week and a half. Then he had to leave, and from there, things would either find a way to work or they wouldn't. William was serious about coming back, but he didn't think they had a chance if Garvin wasn't willing to make an effort. However, Garvin had surprised him before.

"I'll get some drinks." He poured Garvin some coffee and got water for himself. By the time William was done, Garvin had plates on the small table, and they sat down.

"What sort of things would you like to do before you leave? Once this snow is over, the weather is showing a period of quiet for a while, and it's supposed to warm up a little. By Wednesday, it's going to be near freezing. If you like, we could go out on the snowmobile. Or I could see if I can borrow one from Enrique and I could show you how to drive it so we could both have one. There are some great places to ride just to the north. We wouldn't need to go as far as the pass to have some fun. And next weekend is the winter carnival. It's held out on the lake and should be a lot of fun."

"On the lake?" William asked.

"Yes. The lake is relatively shallow, so it freezes deep and fast. The ice is probably four to six feet thick right now."

"That's pretty cool. Do you need to do something for it?"

Garvin nodded. "I'm supposed to help with the kids' games and things like that. We set up the community center as an artists' market and craft show. Clair—she lives in the house three to the west—organizes that each year. The library community room will be used for refreshments, and Enrique always sells food. There will also be native crafts and artists who sell their wares. We have races on the lake of all sorts, even outhouses."

"I take it the carnival is a big deal."

"It is for everyone around here. Most visitors come in the summer, but this is our one big winter draw, and we try to make the very most of it. I can't wait to show it all to you."

"It sounds like fun." William smiled, and Garvin seemed excited. The tension between them seemed to have slipped away, and William was glad for that. He knew the issue hadn't gone away, but he wasn't going to let it taint the rest of the time he had. "So tell me more about how they race outhouses."

Garvin's explanation of outhouses on skis being pushed by teams with an occupant inside, doors flapping open and swinging closed, had William nearly in stitches and Garvin grinning. Damn, that smile made his heart race.

THE FOLLOWING afternoon, Garvin drove them up to the trading post. Enrique joined them and gave William a lesson in driving the snowmobile. Enrique then took charge of Sasha and brought him inside.

Garvin took off with William behind him, being cautious with the speed until William got the hang of the equipment. "Where are we going?"

"It's a surprise," Garvin called back and zipped forward. William followed, glad his goggles were tinted, with the way the sun glistened and sparkled off the undisturbed snowfield. Trees dotted the landscape but then disappeared as they passed the tree line and went up into a pass that seemed completely undisturbed by man. Garvin pulled to a stop at the bottom. William brought himself to a stop right next to him.

"I love it here. This is one of those places that you can only get to by snowmobile in the winter or four-wheeler in the summer. There are no roads."

William slowly turned to take it all in. At the tops of the peaks, the wind blew up clouds of snow that glittered against the blue sky.

"Days like this are rare this time of year."

"What is this place?" It looked like nature's cathedral, with the peaks and the way they sloped down.

"It's one of the many valleys out here. There's a small creek in the center of it, which is why we didn't go all the way to the bottom. It shouldn't be active until the spring runoff, but you never know, and I didn't want to take any chances." Garvin's gaze met William's. "I don't want anything to happen to you."

William swallowed, and then Garvin leaned closer. William did the same, and Garvin kissed him, his lips warm and lush, a complete contrast to the cold air around them. Instantly, heat raced through William, and any chill that might have gotten through his gear vanished. When Garvin pulled back, William was tempted to press for more, but he restrained himself, even as he blinked at the fading intensity of the kiss.

He wished he had words to express how he felt at this moment, with the cold, the heat from Garvin, and their surroundings. William was tempted to challenge Garvin to a race back to the cabin so they could tumble into bed. Instead, Garvin took his hand and held it, and they sat together for a few minutes.

"We should move now," Garvin said. "There's only a few hours of light." William nodded, but Garvin kissed him once more. "Last summer, I packed a tent and came up here thinking I would spend the night."

"Did you?"

Garvin shook his head. "I saw a bear right over there, turned the four-wheeler around, and figured I'd sleep at home. I had no intention of waking up spooned to a grizzly." He grinned as he leaned close once more. "I'd much rather spoon with you. The bear is rough, and those claws...."

"Are you saying you have firsthand experience knowing how bears are hung?" William teased.

Garvin shook his head. "Come on. Let's head back." He started the snowmobile before heading upward to turn around. William followed, and soon they were on their way back down the pass and toward the valley, heading toward the setting sun. His cheeks ached, and William realized it was from smiling so much. He was happy. He never would have thought that being up here, out in the cold, could give him this kind of joy. Of course, he knew a lot of that was the man leading the way home. But still, William couldn't help turning around to take in one last look before they reached the tree line and the unobstructed view of the mountains was gone, tucked away safely behind the trees, waiting for their next visit.

Partway through the way back, Garvin paused. "Are you getting cold?" Without the sun, it seemed colder, but William was warm enough. He shook his head, and they continued their ride back, pulling into the trading post fifteen minutes later.

"Did you have a good ride?" Enrique asked as they parked the snowmobiles. Sasha hurried out, excited to see both of them.

"I did. Thank you. It was amazing." William hugged Enrique before jumping on the back of Garvin's snowmobile, holding him tight, the vibration of the motor stoking the heat that came from deep inside him.

"Are you ready?" Garvin asked. William scooted closer, pressing right to Garvin. "I'd say you are." He molded against him, and William groaned.

"Let's get home. I want a warm bed with you in it," he growled, and Garvin took off, zipping quickly over the snow, with Sasha running behind.

William knew the drill when they got back. He got his gear off and stoked the fire. Then he went to the bedroom with Garvin right behind him, tumbling them both onto the bed.

"That was amazing out there," William said as Garvin kissed him, tugging off William's overshirt and then his pants.

"You know, long underwear may be warm, but it sure as hell isn't sexy," Garvin growled as he tried to get William's off and the dang stuff got caught at his feet. William was afraid Garvin was just going to leave it there dangling off the end of the bed, but with a final pull, it came loose, and Garvin tossed it over his shoulder and pulled off the last of his own clothes.

William sighed as Garvin pressed against him, then pulled up the covers. It was cold, but Garvin engulfed William between his lips, and William gasped. It seemed that he was just as worked up as William, and that was damned fine.

"You don't need to be gentle or slow," William growled.

"I don't?" Garvin asked.

"Fuck no!" William guided Garvin's lips to his, nipping at them as he kissed him hard. "I've been bouncing with an engine vibrating my ass and balls for hours. If you want slow, this ain't the time, trust me." He reached over to the nightstand and grabbed a condom before pressing the foil packet into Garvin's hand.

"I see." He ripped it open and rolled it on, and William wrapped his legs around Garvin's hips.

"What the hell is taking you so—" William gasped. Garvin entered him hard and fast, sending a jolt of energy racing through him.

"Not going to be gentle," Garvin warned, but William pressed against him, pulling Garvin deep. He began to move, William right along with Garvin, wanting him so bad. Their coupling was fast, hot, sweaty, and damned mind-blowing. William held on to Garvin hard enough he might have left bruises. From the way Garvin pounded his ass, William might not sit comfortably for days… and he couldn't care less. All he wanted was Garvin, and he was getting a crash course in the man.

"Don't stop" was all William could muster as the room heated until his entire body felt like it was on fire. Garvin knew just where to touch him.

"I won't, I promise," Garvin told him, withdrawing all the way and then sliding deep inside William, taking his breath away. Then he did it again, sending William into mind-spinning ecstasy. He gripped Garvin tighter, holding him with everything he had.

"Yeah," William groaned when Garvin filled him completely, driving into him. He reached up to stroke himself, but Garvin batted his hand away and gripped William hard, sliding his hand up and down his length to the time of his thrusts. William arched his back, moaning softly as he tried to hold back the tide of passion building higher with each passing second. But the pressure and pleasure were too great, and he flew into his release, painting lines on his belly as Garvin drove deeply into him, pulsing to the beat of William's pounding heart.

OVER THE next few days, William and Garvin developed a routine. In the mornings, while Garvin worked, William brought in wood, read, and watched things on his phone, with Sasha curled up on the sofa next to him. He was going to miss the dog, something he never thought would happen. By noon they often headed out on the snowmobile to the trading post for lunch. Afterward Garvin would finish his workday, and then the two of them were off.

Thursday afternoon it was cold as hell, but clear, so they bundled into Garvin's Jeep and drove north up the Parks Highway for a little over an hour. "Where are we going?"

"You'll see," Garvin said with a grin. The sky was as blue as any William had ever seen, and mountains rose their craggy peaks, covered with snow broken up by black rock peeking through. It was all so ruggedly breathtaking.

William was so busy watching around them that he was surprised when Garvin slowed and pulled off. "This is the Alaska War Memorial."

"We came to see that?" William asked.

Garvin chuckled. "Put your gear on and I'll show you what we came for."

William pulled on his hat and gloves and zipped his coat closed before opening the door. The cold greeted him with its ice tendrils trying to reach everywhere. Still, he got out and waited for Garvin and Sasha.

"Come on." Garvin led the way through the snow to the memorial. "Now, turn around and look down the barrel of the cannon."

William thought Garvin was crazy, but he did, and his mouth fell open. There, right in front of him, in all her glory, was Denali, covered in snow, wind blowing a cloud off the top.

"She's putting on a show just for you."

The mountain was magnificent: snow, ice, and rock, stretching almost four miles toward the sky. "I saw it from over the lake."

"This is probably the best viewing spot in the state. It's rarely out like this. I've passed by here and never seen a thing. The mountain makes its own weather, and she loves to keep herself shrouded in the clouds. But today… she must feel like really showing off."

"I guess." William blinked as he stood watching the mountain. Then they headed back to the car. Garvin turned around, and when William took a final look, he could already see clouds forming near the peak. Within five minutes, the top was shrouded and could no longer be seen.

Garvin turned the Jeep around and they headed south, back toward Willow. "I guess we got really lucky," William said.

"Yes, we did. The mountain only shows herself to those she really wants to. The rest of the time, she shyly hides behind her clouds and mist." Garvin continued south with William watching out the back window as the mountain did indeed cloak herself in the clouds, slowly disappearing from sight.

"Thank you for bringing me here," William said softly. It was like he had gotten to witness something few people did. "I got to see the northern lights, Denali…. What else is there?" He was getting so excited.

"There are glaciers that we could visit at other times of the year, but right now, they're a little difficult to get to, and a lot of the visitor centers are closed until summer. You'll have to come back, and I can take you to see some of them." Garvin seemed happy, and William definitely was. That was the first time Garvin had spoken about William returning like it might actually happen. William definitely took that as a win.

THE REST of the drive back was quiet, especially after the light faded and William let Garvin concentrate on the road ahead. Thankfully it was fairly clear, but ending up in a snowbank was something William did not want to experience again.

Garvin's phone vibrated as they approached the trading post. "Go ahead and answer it for me."

William picked it up from the center console. "This is Garvin's phone."

"William, it's Enrique. I assume Garvin is with you. Can you stop at the trading post? There seems to be a little trouble, and I need your help. I've already called the police, but they're a ways off."

"I'll tell Garvin. We're on our way." William hung up and explained what Enrique said.

"We'll be there in a few minutes." Garvin sped up a little. William held on, thankful it wasn't snowing and the road seemed clear, but there could be ice. Finally they turned off, down the side road, and pulled into the trading post lot.

Garvin hurried out with Sasha right behind him. William followed, wondering what the hell was going on now.

"How dare all of you stick your nose into our business!" someone yelled as William closed the door behind him. Sasha barked and then growled.

"What is going on?" William demanded in his loudest voice, the snap in his tone stopping everyone.

"And you are?" the man asked.

William stood next to Garvin. "I think the real question is, who the heck are you? This is private property, and you have no rights here at all. Now, you can act civil or you can leave. The police have already been called and are on their way." He turned to Enrique and Devon, who seemed overwhelmed. "What seems to be the trouble?"

The loudmouth motioned to the eight men behind him. "You all cost us our jobs."

"I see. And what jobs would those be? The ones at the mine?" Willian got a bunch of nods. "Well, I have news for you. The people who cost you your jobs were the ones blasting in the middle of winter, bringing down half the mountain." He was livid, and Garvin placed a hand on his back. Normally he would have reveled in the touch, but right now, he was so angry he could spit nails. "I saw the mess up there. A huge section of trees was destroyed, and all because someone couldn't follow the rules, or worse. As far as I can see, it was your company that is responsible. And if they laid you off, then we're all sorry for that. But no one here broke the rules." He glared at the men, and one by one, they seemed to take a step back.

"Do you want to leave peacefully or wait until the police get here?" Enrique asked.

The men all shook their heads. "But what do we do about our jobs?" one man asked. "I was counting on that come spring, and now I'll have nothing."

William had no idea what to tell them. This wasn't the fault of these particular people, but it wasn't Enrique's, Devon's, or Garvin's issue to solve. "This has nothing to do with us. We don't have jobs hanging around for you, but neither did we get you fired," Garvin told the group. They all began talking at the same time, and tensions began to flare once more.

"What seems to be the problem?" This time the speaker was Trooper Nelson, as he and another trooper entered the bar area. That began another round of explanations from Enrique and more grousing from the miners. This whole situation would have been funny if William didn't feel for these men and their families. It was like a comedy sketch that went around and around and never got anywhere.

"You all need to go home," Trooper Nelson declared. "If you have grievances, then take it up with the mining company, or the state mining board. They have the real Andrew Greyity to punish the company if they did something against the law. These folks live here, and this is a private business. It's not a forum for you to take out your frustrations or make threats to anyone." He tapped the miners in the back on the shoulders, and they got their gear on and started leaving. Slowly the place emptied out, except for the locals who had come in for a drink or a meal. They'd gotten a floor show tonight.

"This is getting out of hand," Enrique told the troopers.

"Yeah. Well, the mine company terminated everyone, including the three who were caught in the avalanche. It seems they are trying to scapegoat them and make it look like it was all their fault. But I doubt that's the case."

"Were you able to speak to them?" William asked.

Trooper Nelson sighed. "I can't speak about an ongoing investigation."

"I see," William said. "You know, you're a really bad actor. Your eyes give everything away." He stared a second longer and then cut the trooper a break. The leader of the miners was still in the corner, looking puzzled. William left Enrique and Garvin with the trooper and approached the ringleader.

"I won't cause any more trouble," he said without any of the force his voice had earlier.

"Okay." William was about to leave him alone, but he turned. "I have to ask, why did all of you come here in the first place? I mean, you had to know that the people here couldn't get your jobs back for you and that there was nothing anyone here could do to help you. What were you hoping would happen?" He really had no idea what was going through these guys' heads, and it was a little frightening how quickly irrationality could take over.

"I don't know. We all got calls saying that our services were no longer going to be required because the locals had raised a big fuss and the license for the mine was likely to be withdrawn." He seemed more cautious now.

William scratched his head. "You're saying that the company told you that the people here were to blame for you losing your jobs?" He glanced over at Garvin, who finished up with the trooper and joined him. "They tried to blame us for what happened."

"Yeah," the miner said, growing more unsure of his position by the second.

"We had nothing to do with your mine closing. All we did was rescue your fellow miners and try to figure out what happened." William sighed. "And we are all sorry that you won't have a job come spring, but you might think of it this way. What danger were you putting yourself in, working for an outfit like that? They obviously don't care about the people who work for them. If they are trying to cover up what happened, then what other safety issues are they not telling you about?" He held the miner's gaze until he lowered it. "I know you're going to need to find someplace else to work, and I'm sorry for that."

He nodded, pulled on his gear, and left the trading post.

"What was all that?" Garvin seemed as confused as William.

"I'm not sure, but I do know that I'm tired of you all fighting this nameless, faceless company that seems intent on harassing everyone here. This crap needs to stop." William pulled out his phone and sent Arnie a text reminder about the lawyer.

I'm working on it was his response. *Looking for someone with specific experience in Alaska. Got a few leads.* William thanked him and slipped his phone back into his pocket.

"I keep wondering what these people are going to try next," he told Garvin, but there was nothing he could do about it. "Let's go to the cabin." He was tired, and he'd already had enough drama for one day. Who knew that a small village in Alaska could be so exciting?

"Sure." Garvin began putting on his gear while William glanced around the space before his gaze returned to Garvin. "Is something wrong?"

William shook his head, not realizing he had just been standing there. In a few seconds he had come to realize just how much he was going to miss not only Garvin but everyone here when he had to leave. Shit…. Even in his head, he didn't use the word *home* to refer to LA, because whether he wanted to admit it or not, this place with Garvin was quickly coming to feel like the place where he was going to leave his heart behind.

CHAPTER 15

"WHERE'S WILLIAM?" Enrique asked as he and Garvin left the community center. They had done their bit helping with the kids' activities.

"I don't know. He said he was going to check out the carnival, and then he was going to look for me at the outhouse races. William was really fascinated by that idea." Garvin looked over the crowd in the parking area. The fun spilled out onto the lake itself, where the race course had been set up.

"It looks like it's over there and they're getting into position." Devon joined them, and he and Enrique hurried over. Garvin continued looking for William but didn't spot him.

The past week had been quietly intense. Each day that passed brought William that much closer to leaving, and while Garvin hated the idea, he didn't see anything more he could do. He consoled himself that people came to visit and left all the time, but this was different and he knew it. The thought of William leaving left him as cold as his cabin was going to be without William's warmth. Hell, even Sasha was going to miss him something terrible.

Garvin looked around and finally spied William striding out toward the lake. He hurried to catch up to him, and reached the edge of the ice as William approached one of the outhouse teams and then climbed inside the outhouse. Garvin pulled out his phone and took pictures.

The race started, and Garvin switched to video as the outhouses slid across the ice. He kept the camera on William, who grinned and seemed to be having a ball. Garvin found himself laughing as the door to William's outhouse swung closed and then came open again. William hammed it up, reaching for toilet paper as he hung on to the sides.

"Did you find him?" Devon asked from next to him.

Garvin pointed, and Devon cracked up. William looked about ready to fall out, but he caught himself as the outhouse picked up speed.

His team raced toward the finish line and crossed just ahead of the others. William whooped and climbed out, nearly falling as he did.

Garvin hurried over as William and his team high-fived each other. He caught William before he lost his balance again, and hugged him tightly. "I didn't know you were taking part."

"They needed a last-minute replacement," William said, bouncing on his toes. "I can't believe we won." William hugged Garvin hard, spinning them around until Garvin was afraid they were both going to end up on the ice. "That was so much fun. Did you see it all?"

Garvin grinned, happy to his bones. "I did. You even mugged for everyone. I got pictures and video."

"Send it to me. I want to show the guys back in the city. This is the best thing ever." He whooped, and his teammates all joined him before heading up to the stage, where they were presented with their outhouse trophies. One of the men on the lake made them every year. They were outhouse birdhouses, and each one was displayed with pride outside one of the various cabins in the area. "What's next?" William asked as he showed Garvin his outhouse.

"There are more races that we can watch."

"Did you enter any?" William asked.

"Yeah, Garvin," Devon said from behind him. "What race did you enter?"

"None," Garvin groused.

"Wrong. I get my chance to beat you this year. I signed you up for the snowmobile races."

The jerk. Last year Garvin had come in first, but only because one of the other racers had engine trouble and Devon decided to hotdog it and fell off. Garvin's trophy was on a shelf in the cabin, and it made him smile to see it.

"No. You go and win. No hotdogging and shit this year."

"But—"

"I didn't win last year—you lost. Be sure to change that." He sent Devon off and slipped an arm around William, guiding him over to the course. The entrants had to race across the lake, around a cone at the end, and back. The course was about simple speed.

"Go on if you want," William told him, but Garvin tightened his hold a little more. He was fine right where he was. "Does Enrique race too?"

"You better believe it." They watched as Devon won the first heat and Enrique the final one. "This should be good," Garvin said as the four racers lined up for the final race.

"This is the one for all the marbles," the announcer said. "The winner of this race will be the king of winter!" A whoop went up, and then, with a pistol shot, the racers were off.

"Who is leading?" Garvin asked as they tore across the frozen lake. They both watched as Devon's red snowmobile seemed to make the turn first, with Enrique's black-and-yellow one right behind. The others made the turn just after, so it was anybody's race.

The engines grew louder as the racers approached the near side of the lake. "It looks like Devon is just in front." William shouted his encouragement as they drew closer.

"That was a close call, but the king of winter for this year is Enrique Salazar." He drew out the name like it was a boxing match. They all pulled to a stop, and Enrique stood, holding his hands in the air. Devon stood next to him, beaming almost as brightly as if he had won.

"Now that's love," Garvin said softly. "I remember the time I got my first teaching job. You would have thought I'd won the lottery by how happy John was. He took me out to dinner, and the two of us celebrated. It wasn't even a great job."

"But it was your first, and John understood that." William took his hand. "You celebrate along with the ones you love, because if you don't, then the bad things have a chance to overtake you."

"I know you're right, but the bad things, the mean things people say, they're so much easier to believe and harder to let go of. The good stuff seems to come and then it's gone, but the bad things, the hurts, they hang on."

"I know. But they don't have to," William said. "Look at them. They'll remember this day not because Enrique won and Devon lost, but because they were here together. Look at them. All you have to do is see them and you know they're a couple. They watch each other even when the other doesn't know it."

"What are you going on about?" Garvin asked.

William growled at him under his breath. "Look at Devon. He smiles at Enrique even when he can't see it. It's so obvious that he loves the man."

"And I don't? Is that what you're saying? Is this some kind of smile test?" Garvin snapped, and then realized what he'd said.

"Of course not." William leaned closer. "But do you smile at me when I'm not looking?" Garvin cleared his throat. "You do, don't you? Because I know I smile just thinking about you." William lightly bumped his shoulder.

"I see." Garvin didn't know what to say—he hadn't been keeping track of his smiles—but he supposed he did. "I guess I do, because you make me happy." He sighed softly, willing this happy, contented feeling to stay around for as long as possible.

"Come on," William said. "Let's go ride the Ferris wheel. And if you're good, maybe when we reach the top, I'll give you a kiss." He tugged Garvin over and paid for two tickets, and they got in line. Once they boarded the wheel and sat in their seat, William took his hand and scooted as close as possible. "You know, I'm glad I came, even if I did nearly freeze to death."

"I really could have done without that being brought up again. You nearly scared the life out of me that night. I had no idea you were coming, and then you show up at my door, half frozen, nearly giving me a heart attack because…." He paused. "Dammit, I thought I was going to lose you." There, he'd said it. Garvin turned to William as the wheel began to move. Every time they reached the top and crested over, William leaned close and kissed him. Garvin hoped their ride went on forever.

AS MUCH as he might want it to, nothing lasted. Garvin had learned that with John, and he was getting a refresher course with William. The past few days had been great. He taught William how to use snowshoes, and they had been out on the snowmobiles again. Last night, they went to the trading post, and William had said his goodbyes to everyone. Garvin had done his best to put that inevitability out of his mind, but it had been staring him in the face since then.

130

A few hours ago, William had finished packing and they had loaded everything in Garvin's Jeep. Now they were on the outskirts of Anchorage as the last light disappeared from the sky. "It's going to be a cold one." Anchorage got very few clear nights, being so close to the water, but it seemed tonight was going to be one of those.

"I guess so." William turned and smiled. "The northern lights."

Garvin pulled off and parked so they could watch them dance across the sky. "It seems you're getting quite a sendoff."

He continued on, and they stopped for dinner before he took William to the airport, where he pulled up to the departures section to let William get out.

"I promise I'll be back."

Garvin nodded, his throat tight and aching. "I hope you will. Maybe this summer, and we can see all the places we went without the snow." He tried not to get too emotional, but it was becoming harder by the second.

William leaned over and kissed him. "You can always come visit me." He took Garvin's hand. "I don't want this to be the end. It can't be."

"No. Me too." What the fuck did you say at a time like this? "I don't want you to go."

"I know, and I wish I could stay, but I have commitments. But I'll always have room for you and a place for you and Sasha to stay when you want to visit." He kissed Garvin again and then they got out of the Jeep. William got his suitcases out of the back and took them to the curb. Garvin felt his gaze on him as he drew closer, and he hugged William hard. Sometimes words completely failed, and this was one of those moments. Finally, Garvin released William and hurried around to his side of the car. He got inside, buckled his seat belt, and checked the traffic around him before pulling away.

The lights of the airport flashed in the windows, and he was nearly away before he glanced at the passenger window. That was when he saw it—a simple heart drawn in frost outside. Damn it all.

He continued forward, and the light faded and darkness surrounded him. Garvin was tempted to go around the circle, park, and find William to tell him how he felt, but it was too late. Just like with so many things, Garvin had waited too damned long, and now he was out of time.

CHAPTER 16

"CAN WE give that another try?" the director for the commercial William was filming asked. He had been home a week. Arnie had finalized the sponsorship contract, and they were already filming initial spots. It wasn't likely these would actually be used, but management wanted to know how things might look.

William nodded and stepped off the set so the crew could reset. Once they were done, he stepped back into position, smiled, and let the energy he wanted to come across flow through him. Then, when he got his cue, he spoke directly to the camera about how rather than buying frozen pie, you could use this new prebaked crust to make one of your own. It was flaky, buttery, and turned out just like your grandmother made, only in a fraction of the time and without the work and mess. Of course he took a slice out of the most perfect pie known to man, placed it on a plate, and tasted the gelatinous mess, smiling the entire time.

"Perfect!" the director called, and William grabbed a napkin from the set and spat the bite into it before tossing it away. There was no way in hell he was swallowing that. "I loved the energy, and you came across as really genuine."

"Thank you." That was hard, considering the only thing actually tasty on the pie was the crust. Everything else was for the cameras and tasted like glue. "Do you need anything more?" This was the ninth time through, and he was getting tired, but he'd do as many takes as they needed. It was how this job worked.

"No. That's a wrap on this script. Can we do the second one?"

William knew that one as well. Letting the crew set up, he stayed out of the way and spent some time on his phone, checking email and his messages. He hoped there was one from Garvin, but other than a response to the one William sent that he had made it home, it had been largely radio silence. Garvin sent him a few pictures of Sasha, and William responded with pictures of the guys and a few of where he was working, but that was all. He didn't know if Garvin was distancing himself or if the guy just hated texting.

"We're ready for you," the director called.

William stepped onto the set, they walked through the spot, and then they started filming.

Thankfully, the director was happy with the second version after three takes. He dismissed everyone, and William returned to Wardrobe to get out of his costume before putting on his own clothes.

"What the hell was that?" Arnie asked as soon as they were off the studio and in the car. "You were fine on set, but the rest of the time you looked like someone had just killed your dog. What's up with you lately?" He pulled out of the parking garage and onto Santa Monica Boulevard. "You don't seem like yourself."

"I'm fine. I've just been busy since I got back." He settled in the seat, determined not to check his phone yet again. There was probably nothing to see anyway. "The director was happy, and I think the work was good."

"Oh, it was. But it's the rest of the time that I'm worried about. I've known you for years, and it just seemed like your mind was off somewhere else. You know we'll get feedback and changes on the commercials that have to be filmed, and then you leave for Paris in a few weeks. And you're going to need your head in the game for that."

William was well aware of that. Paris Fashion Week was always a brutal test of endurance, without a doubt, and he was going to be scrutinized from the moment he stepped out of his hotel room to until he returned to it.

"The commercials went well, and you know it. They got what they wanted and were very happy. So get off my back." William's tone was sharper than he intended, but he let it be. If it got through to Arnie, then that was what he needed.

"If you think a little snippiness is going to get me to stop worrying about you, then you're crazy." He pulled to a stop at another light. "You've been like this since you got back from Alaska. At first I thought it was because you were tired, but it's more than that."

William didn't want to talk. It was hard realizing your hopes were being dashed in slow motion, and the last person he could tell was Arnie. He hadn't exactly been supportive in the first place. "Did you find a lawyer for me?" He figured changing the subject was a good idea.

"I did. One of the big advocacy groups. The Northern Rockies Conservancy is going to send someone up to speak to your friends. Their mission is to ensure that mining operations are being conducted properly. They have experience, and they know the law. They even have a legal presence in Alaska already. Hopefully they're on the case right now."

William sat back with a sigh, sending Garvin a message about the group. He got a smiley face in return, then a second message. *We have a meeting with them tomorrow. Thank you.*

He blinked at the phone, wondering if that was all he was going to get. He growled under his breath.

"Okay. This is enough. What in the hell did your phone ever do to you?" Arnie asked. "And does it have anything to do with that stick plunged up your backside? This is getting frustrating. What the hell happened up there?" He made the turn into William's building and pulled into a parking space. "Don't think about getting out until you tell me what's going on." Man, Arnie could be feisty. His eyes blazed, and he pursed his cosmetically filled lips.

"Are you sure you want to hear this?" William asked.

Arnie folded his arms over his chest. "Don't make me turn off the air-conditioning."

William smiled and scoffed. "Come on. You'd melt before me." He loved teasing Arnie about his little nips and tucks and the fact that he hated growing older.

Those eyes grew harder, and he didn't take the bait. "Ass," Arnie retorted. "Now spill whatever happened between you and the Alaska man. Did you meet some big bush guy, and did he rock your world to the point that you're going to want to go back there and live off the grid in a tiny shack or something?"

"I know you're teasing. And you met Garvin at a party a couple years ago. He was the one who had lost his husband a few years before. He isn't some bushman, and his cabin is really nice. It's on a lake up there."

Arnie rolled his eyes like he didn't see the difference. "But the rest is true. You fell for the guy, and now he's ghosting you."

"He isn't. Not exactly. He just doesn't talk much. I send him texts and get one-word answers." William shrugged, and Arnie held out his hand. "What?"

"Show me," Arnie said like he was running out of patience. William brought up the texts and handed over his phone. Arnie read through them, shaking his head the whole time. "God. This is like *Lifestyles of the Poor and Boring*." He handed the phone back. "You two are about as interesting as a dead fish. Not everyone knows how to text and not everyone is comfortable with it. If you want to spice up your text life, then you need to be the one to show him the way."

"And how do you suggest I do that?" William asked, wondering if Arnie's cheese had fallen off his cracker.

"Instead of sending him pictures of what's going on around you, send him ones of you, maybe in bed or just getting out of the shower. For God's sake, do not send dick pics—that's gauche and tacky—but if you really like this guy, then give him something to stoke the heat on those cold Alaska nights." He winked, and William felt like smiling, really smiling, for the first time in a while. "Good. Now change that mopey attitude. I'll let you know the schedule for the next set of commercials, and you get yourself ready for Paris. We'll go over your schedule next week. I have four shows booked so far, and there is some additional interest. You also need to be seen in the best light, because while runway shows are important, more and more fashion merchandising is being done online and with video, so I'm hoping to get you launched in that space as well. You have the experience with your other work, so it should be a great opportunity. But this mopey attitude isn't going to do it."

"All right. I'll talk to you soon." William got out of the car. He knew he needed to put this stuff with Garvin out of his mind. He had a job to do, and he was a professional, so it was time to put everything else aside and get on with it.

DAMN, WILLIAM was tired, but the commercials were wrapped up, the folks from P&G were thrilled, and William was on his way to Paris. He loved the city, with all its things to do. Of course there were too many temptations, and if he wanted to look good on the runway under all those lights, those were off limits, especially the food ones. His driver had picked him up on time and taken him to LAX. He'd flown to New York and had most of the day in the city. He got a hotel just so he could get some rest, and while he was there, William took a moment to snap a picture of himself fresh out of the shower and send it to Garvin.

Since his conversation with Arnie, he had indeed spiced up their texting, and it seemed to be working. He got a picture of Garvin in bed, and he even got one of Garvin bare-chested, holding Sasha. William has responded, *lucky dog*.

He also told Garvin he was on his way to Paris and that he'd send plenty of pictures. He didn't get a response right away, but one did come in a few hours later, along with another picture of Garvin, this one cut off in the most tantalizing way. It was sexy as hell.

That evening, he left New York and managed to sleep on the plane. He had learned from experience that he had to rest because he was expected to hit the ground running. At the airport, Arnie waited for him in the back seat of the car that would take William to the hotel. He'd been in Paris for almost a week already and was all smiles.

"Let's get you to the hotel. I managed to book you in an additional show, so you're going to be busy, but it's all good. You're in demand, and that's what we want."

"Really?" He knew he only had a few years left and then he'd just be too old.

"Yes. Of course. Young and pretty will always be in style, but you have a presence the others can only hope for, and that's what these designers want. Someone who will make their clothes look amazing to their customers. Now relax and stop worrying. Everything is under control." He smiled as he sat back, one of those "cat who ate the canary" expressions on his face, and for a second William wondered what the hell Arnie had been up to. "I have your room all ready for you. Here is your key card and the room number. I'm just down the hall if you need anything."

They entered the city, the Eiffel tower jutting into the sky, low buildings covering the landscape all the way to the river.

William had seen this sight before, but it always sent a thrill through him. The car dropped them off out front, and Arnie escorted William inside. "What time do we need to meet?"

"You have nothing until a reception tomorrow evening. A number of the designers you'll be working for will be there. Until then, your time is your own. Go on out and have a little fun." He smiled as they strode through the impressive marble lobby to the elevators. William carried his own luggage and stepped inside the small elevator to ride up to the fifth floor. Arnie pointed William in the direction of his room and then turned the other way.

William had no idea why Arnie was acting strange. He usually spent the first day with William, making sure he knew everything and what time he had to be at each commitment. As he approached the door, his phone dinged with a message. *I added all your commitments to your calendar. Call if you need anything.* It was followed by a smiley face.

Thanks, William texted back, then unlocked the door and went inside.

Garvin lay on the king-size bed, shoes off, his head on one of the pillows, arms folded across his chest.

William couldn't believe his eyes. "When did you get here? How long are you staying? Is this real?"

Garvin chuckled. "It's real. I needed to see you, and I contacted your friend Arnie and asked when you were going to be here. He told me, and I made arrangements. It seems he has been worried about you, and he told me that you haven't been the same since you returned from Alaska. I believe Arnie used the words 'mopey' and 'a real Debbie Downer' to describe your new attitude. He had me call him when I arrived, and he let me into your room a few hours ago." He sat up and then stood and pulled William into his arms.

"This is the best surprise ever," William croaked as he buried his face against Garvin's neck, inhaling his woodsy scent. "It's so good to see you. I missed you so much."

"I missed you too. So did Sasha, who is staying with Devon and Enrique while I'm gone. He moped around the cabin for a week and looked for you every time I opened the door." Garvin held him tighter. "I told you I didn't think I could see you in LA, not yet. But Paris... well, that was a different matter."

William chuckled. "So you flew halfway around the world rather than just down the West Coast." Sometimes people did crazy things. "Doesn't really matter. I'm just so happy you're here." He pulled back and then kissed Garvin hard, pressing him down onto the bed. "I haven't slept well in weeks. It's surprising how quickly I got used to you tossing and turning at night."

Garvin chucked. "And I got used to the way you're always cold."

William kissed Garvin gently, their gazes meeting. "I could be cold now and you could warm me up," he whispered, still having a difficult time believing that this was real. He had dreamed about a moment like this since he'd left Alaska, but he honestly never thought it would happen. His plan was to complete his fashion week engagements, clear things up in LA, and then head back to Alaska for the late spring or early summer. William figured that was the soonest he'd be able to see Garvin again.

"What are you thinking about?" Garvin asked.

"You surprising me like this," William answered. "I didn't expect it at all. Did you do all this because of what Arnie told you?" He could imagine his manager meddling just to make sure William was in the right frame of mind.

"No. I came because I spent nearly two years in my cabin and I was perfectly happy. Then an old friend came to visit and managed to turn everything on its head. All my friends ask about you all the time, Sasha moped for weeks, and last week Devon asked me when you were coming back because he swore my cold, dour expression was delaying the onset of spring." He rolled his eyes.

"I take it neither of us has been particularly happy." William brushed a bit of Garvin's floppy hair out of his eyes. "You need someone to take care of you."

"And you need someone to keep away the grumps." Garvin leaned forward. William's eyes drifted closed as Garvin kissed him, slowly, deeply, rolling him on the bed until Garvin's weight pressed him into the mattress.

"I needed you so many times," William admitted. "I went to the beach to watch the sunset and wished you were there with me. More than once, I turned to the hills in the area but saw that view over the lake." He sighed. "I don't know what we're going to do." Damn, he

138

loved looking up into those deep, incredibly blue eyes. "I have a number of commitments that I have to meet, and they require me to be in LA." There was no way he could ask Garvin to leave Alaska. "But I miss the guys and the sense of community up there. I always felt like I belonged, even though I really didn't."

Garvin drew close enough that his breath tickled over William's lips, and his green-flecked eyes grew wider. William could damned well get lost in those eyes if he allowed himself. "You did belong. Being a part of a place and a community isn't about how long you've known people, it's about caring and being there. You threw yourself into everything from rescuing miners to getting us a good lawyer who has gotten the mining company's license suspended."

William was thrilled about that. "You do realize that we're together again on a damned bed and we're talking about mining rights and snowmobile trips that nearly froze my nuts off. We could put our time together to much better use." He kissed Garvin hard, and passion between them built quickly.

In a matter of minutes the cloud that had hung over William for weeks was gone. He could think again, and all he wanted was Garvin. William tugged at Garvin's shirt as he did the same. Due to mutual squirming, it took longer than he would have liked to get Garvin's shoes off and his shirt over his head. Their breathing came in short, intense pants as William kissed him once more, tugging at Garvin's lower lip as they got each other out of the last of their clothes. It was like they needed reassurance that this was real. William's hands roamed all over Garvin, refamiliarizing themselves with contours that had become so familiar.

"Did you bring stuff?" Garvin whispered.

William grinned. "What stuff? It wasn't like I was expecting anything to happen here. I haven't so much as looked at anyone else. You're all I wanted, and you were supposed to be back in Alaska."

Garvin nodded. "Then it's a good thing I came prepared." He smacked his hand on the bedside table, flashing a foil square, and his gaze grew heated once more. Damn, Garvin knew how to turn him on. There was something in those eyes and the way Garvin touched him that got William's heart racing.

"It's a good thing you did or...." William's words turned to a groan as Garvin slid down him, his tongue blazing a trail over his chest and belly until Garvin slid his lips around his length, taking William all the fucking way. It was like reaching for heaven and getting a touch of it. "Are you trying to kill me?" William mumbled through the haze of passion that clouded his mind.

"I can stop."

William growled from deep in his throat. "Don't you dare."

Garvin chuckled, gripping his cock hard as he sucked it into scorching wet heat. William whimpered, his cries becoming more insistent as Garvin slid two fingers deep inside him. William panted, his nerves firing in so many directions at once that he didn't know what to concentrate on. Eventually he just let it all overtake him and placed himself in Garvin's trusted hands. There was nowhere else he wanted to be, and when Garvin's lips and fingers paused, William opened his eyes, locking onto Garvin's gaze as he rolled on a condom and then slowly entered him, both of them sighing as they came together once more.

"Just like that," William whispered. Garvin knew just how to touch him and how to blow William's mind. He wrapped his legs around Garvin's waist, returning his kisses as he slowly rocked back and forth.

"I know what you want. I remember."

"You also remember that I'm not made of glass." Garvin had decided to go slow, and it just tickled the edges of William's excitement. There were times when William liked things slow, but right now, after weeks apart, everything inside him needed more, *now*.

"I know."

"So quit with the *Driving Miss Daisy* and get with the *Fast and Furious*," William said, holding Garvin's cheeks in his hands. "Give me more."

Garvin smiled, drawing closer, kissing him. "You'll get what I give you, and at the moment, I kind of like you like this: a little frantic, eyes blazing, and your mouth parted like you can't get enough." He kissed him, harder this time and with more urgency, but his pace never picked up. It was frustratingly incredible. Garvin had such control. Most of the time William was a fan, but at this moment, he needed *more* so badly he could taste it. "You look like you're about ready to fly apart."

"I feel like it."

"Just relax. I'm not going to let that happen." Garvin held him tighter. "I came all this way to tell you that you're mine and I'm not going to let you go. I don't know how it is going to work between the two of us." He snapped his hips, sending a zing of pleasure racing through William. "But it will."

He moved his hips faster, and William gasped. "We'll figure it out. I promise. Just like I will never leave you hanging and I'll always do my best to make you happy." Garvin moved more quickly, rocking the bed as he snapped his hips. Skin smacked skin, and William arched his back, giving himself over to Garvin. There was nothing else he could or wanted to do.

"Hell yes," William groaned as the world outside their room fell away. There were no fashion shows, commitments, or anything else to occupy his mind, just Garvin and the way he loved him. "Don't stop."

"Never will," Garvin promised. William's entire body felt like it was on fire. Gaze to gaze, skin to skin, they stayed locked in their incredible dance until William could hold on no longer. Garvin pressed him to the top of passion's mountain, and then with a push, they tumbled off together, coming in a haze that left William spent, exhausted, and feeling more alive than he had in a long time.

He didn't want to move, not that he had the energy. Still, William hugged Garvin to him, not wanting to break this moment. Eventually, Garvin slowly slipped away, only to return with a towel, and after a quick wipe-up, he lay back down with him.

"You know, we could take a nap," Garvin offered.

"Or we can step out of our room and hotel to explore," William offered. "Have you been here before?"

"No."

William groaned as he slowly sat up. "Then we probably need to get something to eat and then hit the town." Suddenly with energy to spare, William got up and tugged Garvin to his feet. "There's plenty of sights that will take your breath away."

Garvin pulled him into his arms. "Nothing will ever be more breathtaking than you."

CHAPTER 17

"ARE YOU sure about this?" Garvin asked. "I figured you would need to get some rest after your flight."

William hurried to the bathroom and started the shower, that tight backside bobbing so invitingly, it was all Garvin could do not to grab him and pull William back onto the bed. "Of course. If I sleep, then I'll end up all mixed up, and I have to be on the top of my game tomorrow night for a reception. So I'll clean up, and then we'll go see the sights. I know a bunch of things that you need to see." He closed the door before poking his head out once more. "Go get ready, and then we'll head out." He closed the door, and Garvin wiped himself down once more before pulling on his clothes.

True to his word, William was showered and dressed in less than fifteen minutes. "Grab a jacket. It's April, and as soon as the sun goes down, it will start to get chilly." Garvin snagged a sweatshirt from his suitcase, and then William was out the door, with Garvin following in the wake of his whirlwind.

"Where are we heading?"

"To the Metro," William answered. They went down in the elevator and out onto the street. A block later, they entered one of the Metro stations, and after getting tickets, were whisked underground to the very center of the city. They climbed the stairs at the other end and found themselves face-to-face with Notre-Dame covered in scaffolding, like a giant stone beast who'd fallen and needed to heal. "It's sad, isn't it? But the cathedral will recover. It's supposed to reopen in 2024."

"Where are you taking me?" Garvin asked. They had been on what seemed like a mad chase until they stood outside another church.

"Here." He paid the entrance fee, and William practically bounced on his heels as he held the interior door open and Garvin stepped into a chapel brimming with light and colors that seemed to fill the very air around them. "This is Sainte-Chapelle. It's a royal chapel, and all this is the largest collection of original medieval stained glass in Europe." William smiled. "I love this place. The light isn't just visual here—you can almost close your eyes and feel it."

Garvin swallowed, looking around as he took it in. Words failed to describe the space. Tall gothic windows soared toward the sky, and light of every imaginable color streamed into the space. "My God."

"Yeah," William said, taking Garvin's hand. "The last time I was here, I thought about experiencing it with someone I cared about."

"How did these survive?" Garvin asked. "It looks so fragile."

William shrugged. "I really don't know. I've been to Paris almost every year since I was twenty-two, and I always come here. It's like my welcome to the city, and it always lifts my spirits. I know it's a church, but it makes me feel like I can do anything. In this space, it's really easy to believe in God and his miracles."

Garvin nodded. They slowly wandered through the monument, taking in the light. He probably should have gotten a brochure to read about the building, but he was too enthralled to take his attention away. Standing in the center, he lifted his gaze. "I can see why they built churches like this. The building itself seems to draw your attention to God."

"That's exactly the point," William whispered. The space was huge, and yet it seemed inappropriate to talk. Garvin wandered silently through the church, taking it all in. As people entered, their chatter ceased at the door, and Garvin knew they were as affected as him.

"We should go," William whispered sometime later, guiding him toward the exit and out into the bright spring sunshine.

"That was amazing," Garvin whispered, heaving in a deep breath. "What's next?"

William took his arm. "Lots of things. We can stroll the booksellers, walk along the west bank." He continued walking, and Garvin let William take the lead. They strolled across the fancy Alexander bridge, where a hunky bronze Neptune held court over the Seine. The city of legend seemed to open herself to them, but maybe it was the other way around. Maybe it was Garvin who was finally opening up. He didn't want to hold back, and when they rounded a bend, looking back as the water flowed through the city, Garvin guided William closer and kissed him hard, his tongue slipping between his lips.

"I don't know exactly what to do," he admitted. "We live completely different lives, and yet here, none of that matters."

"Because maybe it was never all that important in the first place," William offered. "Look, I'm thirty-four, an old man in the business I'm in. The day after tomorrow, I'm going to be in a runway show, and I will be the oldest model there by nearly a decade. I'm good at what I do. And yeah, I look good and I was blessed with young genes. But it isn't going to last forever, I know that. I've worked hard for years, and you know the tiny place I have."

"But the commercials and stuff…," Garvin suggested.

"Those might last longer, for a few more years. But then someone more attractive with fewer lines and signs of aging will take over. It's the way of things. Once that happens, I'll look for a new career." He pulled Garvin nearer. "I have no idea what that will be. Maybe I can teach theater or film. I don't know."

Garvin paused. "What are you trying to tell me?"

William sighed, pausing in their stroll as the river flowed past them the way it had for thousands of years. "That things are not going to stay the way they are now. In four months, I'm booked for some shows in New York. Just a few. Arnie hasn't said anything, but I know it's getting harder and harder for him to get me work. So in a year or two, I'll be ready for a huge life change, and I want that change to be you."

Garvin tilted his head slightly. "You want me to wait for you for two years?"

"No." William looked at him like he was dumb. "I want to come to Alaska and spend time with you between jobs. And I'm hoping that you can come to New York for a few weeks in the fall. You could conduct your classes from there, maybe take your students on a virtual tour of the city. You could come to Paris with me next year, or any other place I have to go. And when this ride is over, then maybe I can find work doing commercials up in the frozen north. Can you see me doing Visit Alaska spots or something?" He smiled, and the light in Garvin's head went on.

"You're saying you'd move to Willow?" Garvin asked, his mouth going dry.

William shook his head. "I've always thought that. I know you leaving isn't an option. That's your home, and quite frankly, it felt more like a home to me than any place has ever felt. I don't know exactly how or when, but the one thing I do know is that I want to make it my home as well."

Garvin rested his head on William's shoulder. "Then I'd love to travel with you for a while, see some more of the world...." He lifted his gaze. "With you. Always with you."

William chuckled.

"I don't understand what's so funny."

William stretched his arm and swept it in front of them. "Millions of people come here every year to fall in love. It's part of what this city does. I think you and I did that in Alaska, but we had to come here to find the words to express it... to figure out a way forward." He kissed Garvin, his lips hot and soft. "You know, if I'd known, I'd have brought you to Paris a long time ago." He sighed. "There's just something about this place that stirs the heart."

Garvin snickered. "I think it's stirring something else, and my bet is that they put something in the water."

William rolled his eyes. "And what would that be exactly?"

"Love juice?" Garvin quipped.

"As I recall, you and I have never had a problem with that." William's wicked smile had Garvin wondering how quickly they could get back to the hotel. Garvin slipped his arm around William's waist, and they stood and watched the water flow past.

"I have to ask. Have you told Arnie about your plans? He seems really intense, and I know the guy works hard as hell for you."

William nodded. "He does, and I'll have to talk to him about it." He leaned closer. "I'm tired, Garvin. By the end of the week, I'm barely going to be able to move. I'll have worn dozens of sets of clothes, and some of them will have been pinned on to the point I'm lucky they don't fall off and I end up naked on the damned runway. That nearly happened five years ago. A new designer hired me for her show. The clothes looked stunning, but they weren't all ready. The pants I was supposed to wear were pinned at the waist, and halfway through the runway, the pin gave way and the pants fell right off." William began laughing, and at first Garvin thought he was kidding, but the chuckle turned nervous.

"What did you do?" Garvin asked.

"I stepped out of the pants, thankful the shirt was long, and continued walking as though that was part of the show. I even gave them a little butt shimmy as I did. The audience never knew anything different, and that designer has hired me every single year since. Last year she started an underwear line for men, and we reprised the pants drop, this time on purpose. It was a sensation. But it takes a lot of energy to be on and ready for those few minutes on the runway, and I want to go out on top rather than trying to hang on too long. You know?" William stood still.

"Do you think you'll be able to get me in to watch some of the shows? I'd like to see you work."

"Of course. Arnie is always invited, and you should be able to go with him." William guided them away from the river. "Let's go a few blocks from this section of the city, find a bistro, and have some lunch."

"I could definitely eat," Garvin said, and they left the riverfront, strolling away from the tourist areas until they found a street corner with a coffee shop on one side and a bistro with tables on the sidewalk on the other. "And afterward, can we walk through the gardens?"

"Of course, if you like. But I thought we'd go to the Orangerie first. It's in one corner of the Tuileries, and it's breathtaking in a completely different way than Sainte-Chapelle." A server approached them. William spoke briefly in French, and Garvin's eyes widened as they were shown to a table.

The bistro was busy but not full, and they settled into a quiet conversation. "I didn't know you spoke French."

"Over the years I've picked up quite a bit, and I took a few years of night classes. When I was younger, I wanted to work more here, so knowing French was important. I'm not fluent, but I can manage most casual situations, and I'm really good in restaurants and things like that because the interactions are predictable." They made their selections and were ready when the server returned.

Garvin sat back and let William speak to the server. Then they were alone, and they simply talked. It wasn't rushed or really important. Garvin spent most of the time watching William, wondering how he could have thought so little of him at one point. He had placed William in a box that made him easy to dismiss, which meant Garvin hadn't had to deal with any latent attraction. All he could do was thank God that

William had come to Alaska. He had opened Garvin's heart again. But it was William's leaving that had been the real wake-up call.

"So, the Orangerie? Why is that familiar?" Garvin asked, trying to pull his thoughts back to the moment rather than letting them wander.

"The Tuileries were the gardens when the Louvre was a royal palace, so I suspect the Orangerie is where they had the hothouses for growing oranges and other tropical fruit for the palace. But today it's something very different."

"And you aren't going to tell me?" Garvin asked.

William shrugged. "You could look it up on your phone, or you can just let yourself be surprised." He cocked his eyebrows, and Garvin left his phone in his pocket. After all, they had plenty of time, and William hadn't steered him wrong yet. The dishes arrived, and Garvin hummed at the simple but amazing plate of duck. It wasn't something he normally ordered, but it tasted wonderful. William seemed content with his chicken, although he only ate part of it and his salad. Garvin kept quiet and just ate, not commenting on the fact that in Alaska, William had had a monster appetite, and now he was eating like a bird.

"I know what you're thinking, and it's because I have to get into those damned clothes in a day or two." He finished his salad, eating slowly.

There were questions Garvin wanted to ask, but he kept them to himself. How much longer did William really want to keep living this way? Watching every scrap of food he ate and wondering if the clothes were going to fit? "I understand, but…."

William shrugged. "I've been doing it so long I don't even realize it anymore."

"Except for when you were staying with me," Garvin whispered.

William nodded. "It felt good to eat whatever I wanted, but it was hell getting my appetite to shrink back down after I got home. I was hungry all the time for weeks."

"Well, if you come back in the winter, you can eat anything you want." He watched William closely for some kind of reaction. Garvin hated this sort of shit. He should just ask for what he wanted, but if William turned him down, then that was it. "Were you happy there?"

William set down his fork. "You know I was." The words came out just above a whisper.

"Then what do you want to do about it?" Garvin sighed. "Look, let's put the bull pucky aside and stop playing games. I was happy, really happy, for the first time since I lost John." He cringed, because the times he had tried running through this conversation in his head, he had said that he was not going to mention John. This had nothing to do with him. "Forget that."

"But John always seems to be there. Even when you say this isn't about him, he's right there."

Garvin nodded. "I know he is, but that's my issue, not yours. Losing John was a big event in my life. It's like Covid—everything seems to be 'before Covid' or 'after Covid.' Well, for me, losing John is that big event, but it's more of a time memory, not like I'm comparing the two of you. Because you and John are like apples and oranges. He was one of a kind, just like you." Garvin cleared his throat and drank from his water, trying to get this back on track before he lost the entire train of thought. "When you came to Alaska, I thought you were going to be a big pain in the ass. But you pitched right in, once you thawed out from nearly being a human popsicle. And damn it all if…." He drew a little closer, losing himself in William's eyes. "You made me fall in love with you."

William gasped softly, his eyes round and huge, like he never expected Garvin to say those words, and maybe he was right, because Garvin never anticipated that he'd use them again, but it was true.

"Then you left, and I got a good dose of just how much you had worked your way into my life. Everyone asked about you, Sasha moped, and I wanted to go to bed and not get up. The entire world seemed to have shifted, and I didn't even realize it until you were gone. I don't want that to happen again."

"Then what do you want?" William asked. He swallowed hard but said nothing more.

"What I want doesn't matter. It's what you want that counts."

William smiled and reached across the table, taking Garvin's hand. "It's what we both want." He lightly rubbed his thumb over the backs of Garvin's fingers. "I have some commitments over the next few months, but after that there isn't a great deal. And I think I'm okay with that."

"I see."

William shook his head. "No, I don't think you do. I'm going to finish my commitments and then find something else to do with my life." He grinned. "I was thinking I could become... a lumberjack or something. I can't just sit on my hands and do nothing. But I can figure that out."

"Then what's stopping you?" Garvin asked, every nerve hyperaware of William's touch. "Wait, it's me?"

William rolled his eyes. "The thing is that you say how I make you feel, but you haven't *done* anything about it."

Garvin's skin tingled from head to toe. Could it be that simple? "Would you move to Alaska and live with me? I know that you would need to travel and stuff, but would you make my little cabin your home... our home?" There, he'd put out there what he wanted. It felt like he had taken a huge leap when all he'd really done was ask for what his heart desired.

William grinned. "I thought you'd never ask."

He shook his head. "But what are you going to do about the deals you do have?"

"I'll finish some of them out while I close up the apartment in LA. My lease is up in a few months. A lot of the stuff there is things I've had for a while, so I'll just sell them and ship up the few things that are really important, like my grandfather's desk and some decorative things. I don't need all that much."

"I was thinking we could expand the one side of the cabin to add an office that could also be a guest room." It was time Garvin reconnected with his friends and had a place for them to stay. Also, since it was going to be more than just him, they would need some workspace. He leaned over the table. "So is that a yes?"

William nodded. "It is, yes." He squeezed Garvin's hand and then released it to pick up his fork. "Finish your lunch. I have something to show you." He checked his phone. "And we have just enough time to eat and get there."

GARVIN WASN'T sure what to expect an hour later as they walked into the Orangerie. Honestly, he was expecting a garden of some sort, maybe a glass house filled with tropical plants. Well, it was a garden of sorts, but a garden of impressionist images that took his breath away: Matisse, Cézanne, Renoir. But it was the elliptical rooms of Monet's Water Lilies that truly transported him. He stood in the center of one room and slowly turned. It was as if he were spending a year in the water garden, the light and color shifting as he turned.

"This is one of my favorite places anywhere," William said softly from next to him. "And to think Monet was nearly blind when he painted these. I like to think of this as the garden of his memories." William took his hand, and Garvin slowly turned toward him. "I used to stand here and wonder what it would feel like to see this with someone else... someone I loved." He squeezed Garvin's fingers before lightly running his fingers down his cheek. They shared a long moment. The gallery, buzzing with people, seemed to quiet, and it was just the two of them. Garvin liked that idea and wished this moment could last forever.

Garvin leaned closer, but William gently shook his head. Still holding hands, they wandered through the rest of the gallery, returning to the water lilies once more before leaving, strolling through the Tuileries as the shadows cast by the trees began to lengthen.

It was under the shade of one of those huge trees that spread its branches wide that William tugged Garvin off the path and onto the grass. "It was too public in there," William said as he stood right in front of Garvin.

"I see," Garvin said as William kissed him gently but deeply.

"I do love you," William whispered. "And I want to try to build a life together. But... you have to promise me one thing."

Garvin raised his eyebrows. "What?" he breathed, wondering what was up now.

"That you'll do your best to keep me warm during the long winter," William said softly.

Drawing close once again, Garvin pressed his lips to William's. "That's something I'll gladly do for a very long time."

CHAPTER 18

WILLIAM STOOD backstage as the designer and one of his assistants fussed over the jacket coat. "It's just not right," the assistant said, frustration in her voice. It was a show for a modern line of formal wear, and the designs were interesting, kicking the black tuxedo up a notch or two with small splashes of color and a highly tailored fit.

"He's too big in the middle," the designer said, and William looked down and glared at him. He had spent years with designers, assistants, casting agents, and God knows who else commenting on his body. Normally it washed right over him.

"No, I'm not. You're trying to stuff me into a coat that is a size too small. My detailed measurements were sent over well ahead of time because I was copied on them." He fixed the designer with a glare before stepping away. "Maybe try that jacket right over there." He pointed, and the assistant raced over.

"Sorry," she said, slipping off the jacket William wore and helping him into the new one, which fit like a glove. "That's perfect."

The designer stepped back. "It really is." He smiled, his eyes softening. Then he nodded slightly, which William took as a silent apology. William did the same and smiled as well.

"I need you to be James Bond all the way, with swagger, confidence, and sophistication. Don't even meet anyone's eyes. Look over them, like you're way above this."

"The ultimate power suit," William said.

"Exactly."

"I can do that in spades," William said, already letting himself slip into character. The designer gave him a final look-over.

"Damn, you sure can. It's perfect." He practically floated to the next model as ten minutes was called. William stayed where he was for the remaining time, except to use the restroom, until they were instructed to line up. He was given the final spot, which suited him fine.

He had long ago stopped being nervous. This wasn't about him but the clothes and the way he could sell them. William knew he looked perfect all the way to the skin. And when it was time, the models each went out and walked the runaway to what began as a modern beat. The first models took the tuxedo in a whole new direction. They were ultramodern, almost club clothes, and if William were younger, he'd definitely have fallen in love with them.

Just offstage, he was paused by the manager as the music shifted to an intense classical music opening that included voices and a beat that shook the room. The handler stepped back, and William walked out onto the runway.

The room was electric, with photo flashes and lights from the sides illuminating every angle and stitch of what he was wearing. William did as he was asked, looking above the back of the room, barely seeing anyone. At the end of the runway, he thought about Garvin and what he intended to do to him when they got back to the hotel. Instantly his smile turned wicked as he opened the buttons and slipped off the jacket, displaying the tailoring on the shirt and the rest of the accessories, including examining his cufflinks.

All that took mere seconds, and then he turned, tossing the jacket over his shoulder, loosened the tie, and popped open the shirt collar. Then and only then did he stride back down the runway in what amounted to a completely different look.

As soon as he stepped backstage, an assistant buttoned up the shirt. Another retied the tie, and then William slipped on the jacket and rebuttoned it just in time for him to do the final walk with everyone else.

This time he kept his smile in place, finding Garvin staring up at him, sitting next to Arnie. William couldn't help a quick wink as he passed, with a photographer catching him at just that moment. The designer joined them on stage to take his bow and applause; then they all returned to the back. Part of William's contract was that he got the keep the clothes, so once he changed, he packed them into a garment bag. When he turned back around, Garvin stood right across from him, his eyes dancing.

"You looked amazing," Garvin whispered. "I mean, in those clothes, you were completely edible." He glanced around. "I have to ask, are you sure you can give this up?" Doubt filled his gaze.

William gathered Garvin into his arms and held him tight before taking a single step back. "This part of my life is winding down. But it's time for a new chapter in my life, and a new direction. And I don't look on it as giving up anything. I look on it as getting something even better: you." Then William cupped Garvin's cheeks, punctuating his point with a kiss.

EPILOGUE

WILLIAM STEPPED out the door of the cabin to a myriad of birds singing in the trees above. Sasha stayed next to him for a few seconds before bounding off in pursuit of some small animal. William was about to call him back but stopped himself. Sasha just wanted to play. He returned, tail wagging wildly, as William continued his trek down to the lake. He stood on the shore, took a deep breath of the cool spring air, and smiled.

Across the lake and to the north, Denali watched over everything. The mountain had become one of William's touchstones over the past year. So much had changed that William didn't even try to recount all of it.

"I figured I'd find you here," Garvin said, draping an arm over William's shoulders.

"This is my morning spot." Even through the past winter, he had come here most mornings just to center himself.

"When do you have to go?" Garvin asked, disappointment in his voice, making William smile in a perverse way.

"I have an afternoon flight Monday," he answered, moving closer to get some of Garvin's warmth. "I'm filming two commercials, and Arnie and I are going to pitch them an idea for the next series. I talked to him yesterday, and we finalized everything. Remember how we used the pie crusts they sent as samples to make campfire pies in the reflector ovens? Well, they're interested in expanding the marketing around building family time."

"And if they go for it?" Garvin asked.

"Then they'd shoot the spots out here in Alaska. And if they say no, then I'll inform them they need to find another spokesperson." He was getting tired of flying back to LA every month for a week to ten days. Inevitably they'd schedule everything, get him down there, and then delays would push back his departure.

"Have you given more thought to what you want to do up here?"

William sighed. "I have a few leads. One of the radio stations might be interested in some voiceover work, and I thought I'd approach the television stations and local companies about commercial work here. I was talking to Enrique and thought we'd devise a 'Come to Willow' campaign to highlight what our area of the state has to offer. There are enough scattered businesses that would benefit, including the perennial farm, the trading post, and a number of outdoor excursion companies and bush tour leaders. This area has a tremendous amount to offer, and it's close to Anchorage."

"Will you be back in time for the hearings in Juneau?"

William turned, gazing into the eyes of the man he adored with everything he had. "Yes. They know that I will not be extending this trip under any circumstances." Last spring, once the snow melted, the full extent of the mining explosion and avalanche had become apparent. Not only was the company negligent in their storage of explosives, but the chemicals they had left on-site had contaminated a large area due to the avalanche spreading the damage farther. Because of the short growing season this far north, it would take decades for the area to recover, if it ever did. "Don't worry about that. I will be there to tell the story of what we found right alongside you. And I have a friend who is going to compile all the video we took of the area into a presentation for the committee. There will be no way they will ever get a license to mine in this state again." Just thinking about the devastation—decades-old downed trees, the river choked with debris, bits of buildings strewn all along the valley floor—he shivered, and Garvin held him closer. The whole idea made him angry enough to spit nails.

"Thank you for all of it," Garvin said.

William smiled brightly. "Of course. I'll do whatever I can. Maybe when I get back, we can make another trip up there to try to clean up more of the mess." They had organized a number of trips to try to clean up the man-made items so that wildlife wasn't injured. The worst was already gone, but there was more work to do.

"We'll see. The snow is still deep up on the pass, but we can take a look at what's left in a month or so." Garvin tugged him closer and then kissed him. It was gentle, but with the promise of heat. He pulled back.

"Good. I want to do what I can," William said, turning his gaze across the lake to the mountain that was already beginning to disappear from view. Garvin sighed softly as a shiver ran through him. "What's wrong?"

"Nothing," Garvin answered quickly. "It's just that sometimes I can't believe that you're here."

William chuckled. "I've lived here full-time since last June, and we just spent an entire winter together in that tiny cabin. If that didn't send me running for the hills...." He smiled.

"I know, and it was amazing, but sometimes I wake up and there you are, and I almost can't believe you're still here."

William turned to Garvin and slipped his arms around his neck. "I'm here because I love this place, and I'm here because I adore you more than life itself." He kissed Garvin hard, loving the way his eyes goggled once he ended it. "Besides, you, Sasha, this place... it's home. And I'll never need anything more." He guided Garvin back toward the cabin. "Now let's go warm you up." He leered heatedly at his sex-on-a-stick partner, thankful it was Saturday.

Keep reading for an excerpt from
Fire and Water
by Andrew Grey.

CHAPTER ONE

RED MARKHAM heard the call for backup through the radio, flipped on the flashing lights of his patrol car, and took off down High Street. He turned north and drove two blocks, going through the stop sign as quickly as he could. Red pulled to a stop behind the other squad car and unfolded himself from the seat. He could see over the hood what the problem was and strode over to where two other officers were struggling with a suspect.

"Get the hell away from me. I wasn't doing nothing!" the suspect yelled at the top of his lungs, trying to yank his arm away from Smith. He managed it, too, and used the free hand to punch Rogers. "You have no right!" Smith got hold of him again. The guy wasn't that large, but he was hopped up on something, that was for sure. When Red caught sight of his eyes, they were as big as saucers, red, dilated, and as wild as a feral cat's.

"That's enough!" Red snapped, wielding his voice like a weapon. The suspect continued struggling.

"Tase him, for God's sake," Rogers called. Smith went for his stun gun, but the suspect knocked his hand away. The situation was turning dangerous fast. Red approached and pulled his weapon.

"Get down now!"

The suspect turned toward him and instantly stopped moving.

"I said get down on the ground!" Red's voice became sharper. Drill sergeants could take lessons from him, or so he'd been told.

The suspect's wide eyes got even bigger somehow, and he stilled completely. Then he dropped to the sidewalk on his stomach and didn't move. "What the hell are you?" the suspect asked under his breath.

Red ignored the comment and kept his gun on the guy while the other two officers cuffed him. Once the suspect was under control, Red put away his weapon.

"Jesus Christ, I'm in the middle of the freak patrol."

"That's plenty out of you," Smith told the prone suspect. "You already have more trouble than you can handle." Smith read him his rights and strongly advised him to keep his mouth shut for the foreseeable future. Red stepped back and glared at the suspect, making sure he made no move toward his fellow officers.

"What happened?" Red asked once the suspect was calm.

"Don't know. He looked strange, and when I stopped to see if he needed help, he went off," Rogers explained. He was a few years older than Red, and they'd joined the Carlisle police force at about the same time. Not that Red knew him all that well, outside of work, or Smith, for that matter. Both men were good guys who Red trusted to have his back when he needed it. But calling either of them friends was a stretch.

"The guy's higher than a kite," Smith chimed in.

"Some new stuff has hit town, and it's strong as hell. This is the second guy like this I've had to deal with, and the department's had about six so far. It's bad and getting worse," Rogers added.

The suspect wasn't moving, and Smith bent down. "Shit, call an ambulance. He's barely breathing."

Rogers radioed in, and within a minute they heard sirens approaching. That was the beauty of a town this size. The ambulance garage was only a mile away, and those guys were always on the ball. Red didn't take his eyes off the suspect in case he was playing possum, but he grew more and more limp. The ambulance arrived, and the EMTs took charge of the suspect, worked on him on the ground, and then got him on a gurney and into the ambulance. Rogers rode along, and Smith prepared to follow in their car, but it didn't look good to Red, not at all.

"Hey, man," Smith said just before they got ready to leave. "Appreciate the help." This whole situation had gone from bad to worse to possibly tragic within about two minutes.

"No problem. I'll see you back at the station." The back doors of the ambulance thunked closed, and Smith went to his car. Red waited until they all drove away before going to his. He sat in the driver's seat and adjusted his rearview mirror. He did not look at himself in it. He never looked in a mirror if he could help it. He knew what he looked like and didn't fucking need to be reminded. He was well aware he was never, ever going to win any beauty contests.

Red snapped out of his thoughts when he heard another call—an altercation at the Y. That was a new one. He responded to the call and was informed that an ambulance was already on its way, along with the fire department. What a fucking day. He wondered for two seconds if it was a full moon, but he didn't believe in all that crap anyway, so he flipped on his lights and hurried to his next call.

The Y was in an old school building that had been expanded. The old part was just that, old, while the addition was new, shiny, and well equipped. Red parked near the ambulance and rescue vehicles. He headed inside and was directed to the pool area. Not that he would have had any trouble figuring out where to go from all the people huddled outside the door. People loved to gawk. "Excuse me," Red said, and some of the people turned around. They stared, the way everyone seemed to stare, and silently got out of the way, tapping others on the shoulder, parting groups of people in workout gear and dripping bathing suits like the Red Sea.

Pushing through the door, Red took in the scene. A woman and a young man in a small red bathing suit stood off to the side. The woman, about thirty or so, Red guessed, soccer-mom type, was yelling and trying to poke the kid in the chest. One of the firemen was trying to separate them and looked grateful when Red approached.

"What's going on?" His voice echoed off the walls of the natatorium.

The woman stopped still, and the kid took a step back, nearly falling into the pool. "He…." the woman began, regaining her composure. "He nearly killed my son."

"I did not, lady," the kid protested, crossing his arms over his sculpted chest. Red quickly took him in and swallowed hard. He was a specimen of damn near perfect manhood, like he belonged on the cover of some magazine. He allowed the thought for a split second. "If you'd have been watching your son and making sure he obeyed the rules the way you're supposed to, none of this would have happened."

"All right. You, over there." Red pointed to the kid. "Sit down, and wait for me." Red then turned to the woman. "You, follow me." He took a step back and waited for both of them to obey his instructions. "Sit here, and I'll be with you in a minute." He waited for her to do as she was told and walked over to where a young boy lay on the tile around the pool.

The kid was blue, and Red watched as two EMTs tried to resuscitate him. It didn't look good, but then the kid coughed, spit up water, and gasped for air. Red motioned to the woman, and she hurried over. The boy, who looked about eight, coughed again, and the paramedics told him to stay still. His mother rushed to him, and he began to cry.

"You're going to be all right," the paramedic said to him. Red had crossed paths with Arthur before and knew he knew his stuff. "Just rest and breathe."

"Mom," the kid said.

She took his hand. "You're all right," she soothed, and then she began thanking the people who'd helped her son.

"We're going to take him to the hospital so we can check him out," Arthur told the woman. She nodded and didn't release her son's hand.

"Ma'am, I need to speak with you," Red told her. She nodded and whispered to her son before getting up and walking over to where Red waited. "What happened?"

"I didn't see it. I had dropped Connor off for his swimming lesson, and he was going to stay for open swim afterwards. He and his friends usually do. I got here and saw them pulling him out of the water. I called the police." She turned toward the lifeguard, who sat where Red had told him to. He looked nervous as hell. "I only know that if he'd been doing his job, none of this would have happened," she spat.

Red pulled out his pad and began writing down what she had told him. He got her name, Mary Robinson. He also got her address, telephone number, her date of birth, along with Connor's, and all other pertinent information. "So just to be clear, you didn't see exactly what happened?"

"No, but…." Her argument had rung hollow, and it looked like it was starting to sound that way to her as well. She looked toward her son. Red noticed that she was looking anywhere other than at him. It was something he'd gotten used to.

"It's all right. We'll find out what happened."

She kept looking at her son, and Red stepped back to let her be with him. Then he walked over to where the lifeguard sat on the bottom row of a set of bleachers set up along the side of the pool so spectators could watch races.

Red saw the startled expression on the kid's face as he approached. The kid did a better job than most of covering the pity Red saw flash through his eyes for a split second. "Can you tell me your name, please?" Red asked, getting things moving.

"Terry Baumgartner," he answered, swallowing hard. "He and his friends were horsing around on the pool deck. I told them more than once to stop and was about to ask them to leave when I turned away because a little girl had approached my seat. And when I looked back, I saw him under the water. I dove in, along with Julie." He motioned to the young woman in a red one-piece swimsuit who stood a little ways away. "I reached him first and pulled him out. We started resuscitation right away and continued until we were relieved a few minutes later."

"Who called this in?" Red asked.

A man stepped forward. "I did. They yelled to call 911, so I did. The kids were roughhousing, and I remember thinking someone was going to get hurt."

"Daddy, is Connor going to be okay?" a little girl in a wet bathing suit asked as she walked up and took the man's hand.

"Yes, honey, he's going to be fine," he said, soothing the kid's fears before turning back to Red. He swallowed as he met Red's eyes. Very few people did that anymore. "What he said is the truth. The kids were asking for trouble. If the lifeguard did anything wrong, it was not kicking them out earlier. But he did warn them."

Red glanced to Terry, who nodded. Some of the worry seemed to slip from his aqua eyes, and his godlike, lanky body lost some of its tension. He lowered his lean arms and let them hang down from his sculpted shoulders. Damn—the kid wasn't big, but he was perfect, as far as Red was concerned. "Thank you," Red said, turning back to the man. He took down his contact information and asked a few more questions before thanking him again. He then talked to the other lifeguard, Julie, who confirmed what Terry had told him. Red was satisfied that this was an accident and that the lifeguard hadn't been responsible. He then spoke with the manager of the facility and got the necessary information from him. He was very helpful and seemed concerned and relieved at the same time.

By the time Red was done, Connor had been taken to the hospital, and most everyone else had been dismissed. He was getting ready to leave when he saw Terry and Julie standing off to one side, talking animatedly back and forth. Their voices weren't as quiet as he assumed they meant them to be, because he heard little snippets of their conversation. "I'd die if that happened to me," he heard Terry say and saw the kid looking his way. Red ignored him and walked carefully over the wet tile toward the door. Beauty was only skin deep.

"Red." He turned and saw Arthur approaching. He'd obviously heard what was being said as well. "Don't listen to them. That kid is as shallow as an overturned saucer." Arthur said it a little louder than necessary, and the chatter from the corner ceased abruptly. "When you get off tonight, you want to meet us at Hanover Grille?" he asked more softly. "Some of us are going to have some dinner and hang out for a while. You're welcome to join us, you know that."

Red smiled slightly. He was self-conscious about his smile, and when it threatened to go wider, he put his hand in front of his mouth. "Thanks." His impulse was to say no, thank you, and just go home after work, but Arthur was sincere, and it might be good to get out with people for a change. "Once I'm off shift and get my reports done, I'll try to stop by. It may be late, though."

"I know how things work," Arthur said, and then he hurried away, out of the natatorium.

Red did a mental check that he had spoken to everyone and had all the information he needed. He confirmed he had, and when he checked the clock on the wall, he said a silent thank-you and left the building.

As soon as he pushed open the outside door, he saw four news vans out front, with reporters milling around getting ready to file their stories. Red went right to his car and left, even as they were making their way over. He had no intention of making any comments to the press. He would head back to the station and let the powers that be decide who they wanted to speak for the department.

He got back to the station and filled in the captain about both the suspect on the sidewalk and the near drowning. He made sure the captain knew about the reporters and then headed to his desk to start writing reports. It took an hour. He filed them and got ready to leave. It had been a long, exciting day, and he was exhausted. Red didn't talk much with the other officers in the station. He did say good-bye to the ones he encountered, to be polite, and then hurried to leave.

Red was already in his car and pulling out of the lot when he remembered Arthur's invitation. Since he didn't have anything to do this evening besides sit at home, watch television, and drink too much beer, he decided to take Arthur up on his offer.

SCAN THE QR CODE
BELOW TO ORDER!

ANDREW GREY is the Andrew Grey of more than two hundred works of Contemporary Gay Romantic fiction, including an Amazon Editors Best Romance of 2023. After twenty-seven years in corporate America, he has now settled down in Central Pennsylvania with his husband of more than twenty-five years, Dominic, and his laptop. An interesting ménage. Andrew grew up in western Michigan with a father who lovedto tell stories and a mother who loved to read them. Since then he has lived throughout the country and traveled throughout the world. He is a recipient of the RWA Centennial Award, has a master's degree from the University of Wisconsin–Milwaukee, and now writes full-time. Andrew's hobbies include collecting antiques, gardening, and leaving his dirty dishes anywhere but in the sink (particularly when writing). He considers himself blessed with an accepting family, fantastic friends, and the world's most supportive and loving partner. Andrew currently lives in beautiful, historic Carlisle, Pennsylvania.

Email:andrewgrey@comcast.net

Website:www.andrewgreybooks.com

Follow me on BookBub

THROUGH the FLAMES
ANDREW GREY

Carlisle
Fire

1

Carlisle Fire: Book One

Kyle Wilson hasn't had it easy. His insecurities and nasty home life made him lash out as a kid, and when he finally came out as gay, his family disowned him. Then, just when he's pulled his life together and gotten his construction company running, he's caught in a fire and forced to take costly time off.

When firefighter Hayden Walters rescues a man from a burning building, he's just doing his job. He doesn't expect it to turn his life upside-down, but the man is none other than Hayden's high school bully.

He definitely doesn't expect Kyle to come to the station to thank him in person.

With awkward apologies out of the way, Kyle and Hayden realize they have a lot in common. And when it turns out someone set the fire at Kyle's construction site to target him, they find they can solve each other's problems too: Hayden needs a place to stay while his apartment is renovated, and Kyle doesn't want to be alone in case the firebug strikes again. Things between the two of them quickly heat up—but so does the arsonist's agenda. Can they track down the would-be killer before it's too late?

SCAN THE QR CODE
BELOW TO ORDER!

ONLY THE BRIGHTEST STARS

ANDREW GREY

The problem with being an actor on top of the world is that you have a long way to fall.

Logan Steele is miserable. Hollywood life is dragging him down. Drugs, men, and booze are all too easy. Pulling himself out of his self-destructive spiral, not so much.

Brit Stimple does whatever he can to pay the bills. Right now that means editing porn. But Brit knows he has the talent to make it big, and he gets his break one night when Logan sees him perform on stage.

When Logan arranges for an opportunity for Brit to prove his talent, Brit's whole life turns around. Brit's talent shines brightly for all to see, and he brings joy and love to Logan's life and stability to his out-of-control lifestyle. Unfortunately, not everyone is happy for Logan, and as Brit's star rises, Logan's demons marshal forces to try to tear the new lovers apart.

SCAN THE QR CODE BELOW TO ORDER!

HEARTWARD

Heartward: Book One

He doesn't know that home is where his heart will be....

Firefighter Tyler Banik has seen his share of adventure while working disaster relief with the Red Cross. But now that he's adopted Abey, he's ready to leave the danger behind and put down roots. That means returning to his hometown—where the last thing he anticipates is falling for his high school nemesis.

Alan Pettaprin isn't the boy he used to be. As a business owner and council member, he's working hard to improve life in Scottville for everyone. Nobody is more surprised than Alan when Tyler returns, but he's glad. For him, it's a chance to set things right. Little does he guess he and Tyler will find the missing pieces of themselves in each other. Old rivalries are left in the ashes, passion burns bright, and the possibility for a future together stretches in front of them....

But not everyone in town is glad to see Tyler return....

SCAN THE QR CODE BELOW TO ORDER!

ANDREW
GREY

A HEARTWARD
NOVEL

HOMEWARD

Heartward: Book Two

Second chances only happen in the movies... right?

For the past several years, Matthew's life has been one challenge after another. Keeping his sister's four orphaned kids fed, clothed, housed, and entertained has him run ragged. Now he's losing the kids' mentor and maybe his job, if the plant where he works as an electrician shuts down like the rumors say. When his car won't start outside the hospital, it's the last thing he needs. Matthew could use a hero... so of course that's when Lucas Reardon shows up again.

A-list actor Lucas Reardon returned to his Michigan hometown to say goodbye to his father. The last person he expects to see is Matthew Wilson, the one who got away. Lucas helps Matthew out with the car, the kids, whatever he needs. But really, *he's* the one who needs saving. Years of the fast-paced Hollywood life have worn him down to nothing, and a deranged stalker is making his life hell. Matthew becomes his refuge. But relationships need time to grow and bloom. With the paparazzi breathing down their necks and a deadline on Lucas's return to LA, can they build a life worthy of the big screen?

SCAN THE QR CODE
BELOW TO ORDER!